"Admit it, lady!"

Cal's tone was firm as he placed his hands on her shoulders.

"Admit what?" Marlo asked defensively.

"That you've been lusting after me from the beginning." His blue eyes sparked with mischief . . . and desire.

"How can you say such a thing?" Marlo moaned, ducking her head in embarrassment.

"Easily." He yanked away the cushion she was clutching and drew her close. "You just need to admit it to yourself."

"Why should I?" Marlo mumbled from the warm hardness of his chest.

"Because then we could make love all night long. . . ."

Like all red-blooded American women, **Helen Conrad** has always had a special place in her heart for the laconic Western hero. And Cal James, the sexy, blue-jeaned cowboy in *Diamond in the Rough*— Helen's second Temptation—is the composite of all her dreams. Ms Conrad, who also writes as Raye Morgan, is a native Californian who grew up in Holland and the Pacific island of Guam. She now makes her home in the Los Angeles area with her husband, Rae, and four very energetic young sons.

Books by Helen Conrad

HARLEQUIN TEMPTATION
3–EVERLASTING

HARLEQUIN ROMANCE
2731–TEARS OF GOLD

These books may be available at your local bookseller.

Don't miss any of our special offers. Write to us at the following address for information on our newest releases.

Harlequin Reader Service
901 Fuhrmann Blvd., P.O. Box 1397, Buffalo, NY 14240
Canadian address: P.O. Box 603,
Fort Erie, Ont. L2A 9Z9

Diamond in the Rough

HELEN CONRAD

Harlequin Books

TORONTO • NEW YORK • LONDON
AMSTERDAM • PARIS • SYDNEY • HAMBURG
STOCKHOLM • ATHENS • TOKYO • MILAN

Published August 1986

ISBN 0-373-25218-8

Printed in Canada

1

"LOOK!" JERI CRIED dramatically, throwing open the door of Marlo's office. "Look what I found!"

Marlo Santee closed her eyes for just a second, not sure she was ready to face another of Jeri's bright ideas. It had been a long day. In fact, it had been a long week. Her head was throbbing. She was way behind schedule on the Caron account, and she had a meeting with her boss, Art Grayson, head of Grayson's Advertising Agency, in less than an hour—a meeting at which she would again have to defend a position that was getting harder and harder to justify. And here was Jeri with yet another "answer to all her prayers." She wasn't sure she could take it right now.

She sighed, raising her head from the paperwork on her desk. But then she took in the object of Jeri's jubilation and stopped short. Jeri'd brought in a man. A very large, seemingly reluctant man. And Marlo knew exactly why she'd brought him.

Marlo appreciated her assistant's flair for the unexpected. It often came in handy. She was more cautious herself, her soft gray eyes always appraising, her pretty face often creased with a slightly anxious frown.

"Hmmm," she murmured, tilting her head to the side and tapping her pencil against the side of her nose. She looked the man up and down, impressed almost against her will. Her headache was forgotten.

Jeri grinned. "What do you think? Don't I always come through for you, boss?" She was fairly bouncing across the office in her excitement, her tiny, compact body bristling with energy. She'd been Marlo's assistant from the first and Marlo treasured her, even if she sometimes despaired of keeping up with her overflowing exuberance. Jeri's brown hair was cut short, and her blue eyes danced with life. Marlo had often said she looked like a forest elf with a little acorn cap on her head. "What do you think?" she insisted.

Marlo rose slowly from her chair, staring hard. She'd been searching for the perfect man for a very important series of ads, a series that would probably decide her future in the advertising business. She'd spent days looking over candidates, growing more and more desperate. Here she was in Los Angeles, the entertainment capital of the world, a town full of every sort of male animal imaginable, and she couldn't find what she needed. She'd had men parading through her office, one after another, until she felt as though she'd scrutinized the entire male population of the state.

It had been fun at first. She and Jeri had managed to keep up a good professional front, only to collapse in giggles when the door closed on the gorgeous hunks the casting agencies sent them, men who preened and pranced and turned on the charm, hoping to win a job. But the fun had diminished as group after group made its entrance, only to be turned away. She just couldn't find a man to fit the image she had in mind, the image she couldn't put into words, but could see every time she closed her eyes. She'd just about given up. Weren't there any real men left in the world?

Now there was this one. He wasn't exactly what she'd imagined, but there was something about him.

"You know," she said reflectively, walking toward him, "I think…" Her voice trailed off as she looked him over. She didn't want to go out on a limb until she was sure. "He's certainly tall enough," she ventured, her gaze traveling along the rangy length of him. "Wide shoulders," she added, reaching up to tap one of them with her pencil.

"Yeah, yeah," Jeri agreed impatiently. "And slim hips and muscular thighs and all the rest." She glanced at where the man stood, his legs spread wide in their worn denim jeans, his thumbs hooked into the leather belt with the huge piece of turquoise at the buckle, his denim vest hanging open over the brown plaid shirt with the mother-of-pearl snaps. "The body is great. But bodies are a dime a dozen. We've seen two hundred and fifty who are just as good in the past few days." She leaned closer, her smile sparkling. "It's the eyes. Look at the eyes."

For some reason Marlo hesitated to do that, and suddenly she realized she'd been instinctively avoiding the man's eyes from the first. "I like the boots," she commented evasively, nodding toward the carpeted floor. The leather had once been finely tooled, but now looked scuffed and authentically worn. "There's nothing 'urban cowboy' about the way they look."

"The eyes," Jeri hissed, jabbing her with an insistent finger. "Look at them."

Marlo pushed her long black hair away from her face in a characteristic gesture, then raised her chin and met the cowboy's eyes. Yes, she'd been wise to avoid them. They were dark blue, hooded, staring at her with an assessing arrogance that set her nerves on edge. There was none of the eagerness to please she usually saw in a male model's eyes, none of the sultry provocativeness designed to turn her head. If she hadn't known better, she'd have thought he was the one interviewing her.

She looked away quickly, not sure why Jeri thought those eyes were so wonderful. But in the meantime she took in the rest of his face, and then she knew. He looked about thirty-five. His features were bold and jutting, his eyebrows thick and dark, as was the mustache that shielded his mouth. His nose was straight, his cheekbones wide. There was the faintest suggestion of a cleft in his chin, and the rest of the jaw could have been chiseled from stone. It was a face honed by experience, not all of it pleasant. This was no smooth-faced pretty boy trying to make it in Hollywood. This was a man who'd been around.

Yet he was handsome in a hard-edged way. The hair could have used a cut. Light brown streaked with blond like wood aged in a desert sun, it was thick and wiry and sprang about his head as though he'd just ridden hell-for-leather across a prairie. And that was the best part. Everything about him looked that way. His skin was darkly tanned, yet glowing with a natural health. After a week of looking over smoothly handsome men whose skin color came from a bottle or a sunlamp, Jeri seemed to have finally found what she needed—the genuine article.

So why was she hesitating?

"No Stetson?" she murmured vaguely, knowing this man was the closest thing yet to what she had in mind and only wishing she could join in Jeri's enthusiasm. Some little instinct was sounding an alarm she couldn't ignore.

"He didn't have one on when I found him," Jeri said, "But I'm sure I could round one up if you want to get the full effect."

Marlo knew they were talking about the man as though he was some sort of inanimate object, as though there was no mind to go with the body. They did it partly out of habit—when working with male models that often seemed the case—but she knew there was more to it. If she talked to him, she'd have to look into his eyes again, and for some illogical reason she didn't want to do that.

"Where did you find him?" she asked coolly, straightening her shoulders in an unconscious effort to harden her image—a defense against something unseen but sensed.

"He was coming off the elevator with a bunch of other models. I guess the Media Center had sent for them, but I grabbed him as soon as I saw him. I knew you wouldn't want anyone else getting him first, not when you have such a good idea for the Caron ad." She danced on her toes. "Isn't he perfect?"

Marlo hesitated, then nodded quickly. "Yes," she had to agree, "he seems . . . almost perfect." Why didn't the man say anything himself? Maybe he was just another dumb clotheshorse, despite what she'd seen in his dark eyes.

"What's your name, cowboy?" she asked, then sent him a glinting glance before she moved back behind the desk.

"James." His voice was crisp and deep, with just enough of a drawl to fit in with his Western image.

Western image! And he called himself James? She couldn't hide a smile. "Don't tell me, let me guess. First name Jesse?"

"Nope." His expression didn't change. "Cal."

"Cal?"

"Short for California."

"California James?" She'd never heard anything so ridiculous in all her life, and she didn't believe it for a moment. But what the heck. If he wanted to make up his own stage name, why not? Everyone else in this town did the same thing.

"Let's see how you move, Cal. How about walking across the room for me?"

She turned and met his gaze, her own calm and firm. She saw something new in his, a shimmering reaction that might have been amusement.

"Just what kind of a walk did you have in mind, ma'am?" he asked softly.

She found herself tugging at her lower lip with her teeth. "What kind of walk do you do?" she shot back.

Now he was almost grinning. "That depends on what you want. I can mosey." Though he didn't take a step, his body relaxed in a way that brought to mind that very style. "I can stroll. I can walk bowlegged as a cowboy just in from a month on a cattle drive, or I can give you the steps to a Texas hoedown." He was definitely grinning now. She wasn't sure if he were making fun of her or himself. "You name it, ma'am. I'll try my best."

Why was she getting the idea that the thick drawl was just a little exaggerated, as though he were teasing her? She narrowed her eyes, trying to see into his mind through his expression. "If you'd . . . just take a few steps . . ." she began uncertainly, but then Jeri saved the day.

"I know," she said, taking charge, "why don't we try this." She dragged a chair out from the side of the room. "Straddle this chair, leaning against the back as though you were leaning against the horn of a saddle. We just want to get an idea of what you'll look like."

Marlo saw him hesitate, then glance at the gold watch on his wrist before complying. But she didn't stop to wonder about the gesture. She was too busy noting his easy grace as he swung his leg across the chair as though mounting a horse. She didn't have to see him walk. She already knew he moved like a mountain lion prowling his territory.

"Is this what you want?" he asked, leaning forward and looking up with a faintly quizzical, amused expression.

Jeri grabbed her own throat with two hands. "Oh my gosh, would you look at him? Tom Selleck, make way. We could sell posters of this guy, I'm telling you, Marlo."

A strange tug-of-war was taking place inside Marlo. Intellectually she agreed with everything Jeri was saying. But something in her resisted it. Something in her was saying, "No, stop. Don't let this happen." She frowned, wondering why.

Maybe it was just that she was afraid. After all, a decision here would affect her in so many ways. Was she hesitating now for fear of another failure? She couldn't let that paralyze her. This man was the closest she'd found to what she wanted. It was about time to take the plunge.

She put a hand to her forehead and turned away, trying to think. Standing against the backdrop of the Los Angeles skyline, she made a lonely picture as she wrestled with her judgment. She wore her thick black hair long and loose today, its silky bulk falling well below her shoulder blades. Her heart-shaped face would have been called sweet except for the constant line between her feathered eyebrows that told of a vague anxiety haunting her. At twenty-eight she'd seen her own measure of life, though her experience had been limited somewhat by her natural reserve and cautious nature. She was good at what she did, and she worked hard at it. She'd had her share of success, especially in Chicago. But somehow it was never enough to erase the failures of the past. And here in Los Angeles the success hadn't come. The harder she worked, the more it eluded her, dredging up old ghosts that would be better laid to rest.

Blocking out thoughts of misjudgment, she raised her chin and swung around. No more uncertainty. She'd made up her mind. "Okay, Cal," she said abruptly, digging through the papers on her desk, "we're interested. Do you have a union card?"

"Nope."

"Well, you'll need one for this job, but we won't worry about that now. Jeri is a genius at getting that sort of detail straightened out." She bit her lip and looked down at her desk. "Here are the thumbnails, if you'd like to take a look and get an idea of the mood we're aiming for. If this works out, it could get you television commercials as well as the magazine ads. Whoever we pick will be the Caron Man and will go under exclusive contract for at least six months. Subject to the okay of the client, of course." She risked a hesitant glance at him. "You don't seem to have your composites with you. What kind of work have you done before this?"

She looked at him again, and that was a mistake. She could have sworn he was laughing at her. He covered it up quickly, but the laughter had been there, surging behind the rich dark luster of his eyes. What on earth was so funny?

She forced herself to hold his gaze this time, staring him down. If she were going to be the boss on this project, she'd better establish that from the first. She didn't need any more problems. She had enough of those already, what with Art Grayson acting very hard to please and Mr. Caron in a state of near hysteria. Why should she hire someone who was going to add to her burden?

The cowboy seemed to read her mind. He rose from his chair and walked slowly over, sitting on the corner of her desk in a way she found unnecessarily familiar. Only then did he answer her question about previous work. "I guess you might say I'm a greenhorn," he told her silkily. "You'd be my very first."

She blinked at him, then looked down at the papers again. A little rush of relief surged through her. Maybe it was a sign. It was certainly an excuse. "No experience," she said evenly. "I don't know, Jeri...."

"What?" Jeri cried, catching her drift right away. "Are you kidding? You're not going to let the perfect man walk away just because he's never worked in the business before!" She waved a hand his way. "He's the most outdoorsy, masculine thing we've seen all week, and that's exactly what you said you wanted."

"I know, but we also need someone who knows what he's doing. This is a major account."

"He knows what he's doing." She turned on the man, her blue eyes snapping. "Show her. Do something outdoorsy. Do something masculine."

His shrug was dangerously lazy, and Marlo had a bad feeling about it right away. She stood at the same time he did, and she barely heard him saying "I guess this is about the most masculine thing I know how to do," before his hands were on her shoulders and her face was tilted up, gaping in surprise.

He kissed her. The man who was applying for a job as the model for an ad campaign kissed the account executive to prove he could do the job. Another time she might have laughed at the absurdity of it all, but at that moment she didn't see the humor.

He kissed her and, even stranger than that, she let him. It was the shock, she told herself later. She was so astonished she was frozen to the spot. And so his lips touched hers, feeling softer than she would have imagined, silky smooth and tender. The mustache tickled only a little. Then he was gone and the pressure of his hands on her shoulders was gone, too, and she was still staring at him, still stunned.

"Was that masculine enough for you?" he asked, and when she didn't answer right away, he chuckled. "Maybe I'm out of practice," he said. "Sorry about that." He hitched up his shoulders in a way that told Marlo he meant to leave, and she still couldn't think of a thing to say. "Well, this has really been fun, ladies," he said casually, turning to include an uncharacteristically speechless Jeri in his remarks. "But I'm afraid I don't have time for any more." He started toward the door.

Jeri was the first to come back to her senses. She rushed around him and tried to block his way. "Where are you going?" she cried. "You've convinced her. Believe me. I know."

"I'm not so sure." He glanced back at Marlo and shook his head ruefully. "She doesn't seem convinced to me."

"Mr. James," Marlo said as firmly as she could considering the way her head was spinning, "you—you are an unconventional man. I'm not sure . . ."

He grinned at her and went back to the exaggerated accent. "Don't worry about it, ma'am. I wasn't hankerin' after this job anyway. I got me some other things I gotta do."

"We'll pay you more," Jeri insisted, grabbing his elbow as he tried to get past her. "Tell him, Marlo!"

He looked down at her and laughed a long, low, rich laugh that seemed to fill the room. "I'm not a model, lady. I'm just a poor innocent cowpoke in the wrong place at the wrong time." He gently pried her fingers from his arm.

"Then why . . . what . . ." Marlo stepped around the desk and came after him, too.

He watched her, his eyes still haunted by that strange sense of appraisal he'd had from the first. But something else was there, too, a sort of melancholy regret that piqued her curiosity.

"I rode up in an elevator full of models," he explained, "and when I got out, this little pixie with the iron grip grabbed hold of me, yelling 'Eureka!' and dragged me down the corridor." He grinned at Jeri. "I couldn't help but be curious as to what she was all about." He glanced back at Marlo, his gaze darkening. "And then I saw you," he said softly, making her feel that strange sense of foreboding again, but he went on as though the words had been unspoken. "I'd never been called perfect before." He smiled. "I knew I was good, but perfect—heck, I feel like a new man."

"You're not interested in doing the ad?" Marlo asked. Suddenly she was sure he was the man she needed.

"No." He shook his head decisively. "Offer it to someone who needs the work." He winked at Jeri and gave Marlo only the trace of a smile. "Sorry I wasted your time. Hope you have better luck with your next prospect."

Then he was out the door, and Marlo and Jeri were staring at each other, horror-struck.

"Do something," Jeri cried, throwing up her hands. "Did you see the way he looked at you? You can get him back if you try."

To her own amazement Marlo found herself racing through the outer office and into the corridor, hurrying after the cowboy as he made his way to the directory next to the elevator.

"Mr. James," she called, and he turned, watching her come up to him, his face expressionless. "Mr. James, please . . ." She was wondering why she was there. "If you should change your mind . . ." She dug into her pocket and presented him with her card. "Here's my name and number. Please call me if you decide you'd like to be the Caron Man for us."

He looked at the card without taking it, then looked at her, a bemused smile just barely curling the ends of his mustache. "Does that mean you'd hire me?" he asked.

She opened her mouth to answer, then closed it again. Looking into this man's gaze was like peering into a crystal ball filled with misty promise and hazy memories. She wasn't sure why he disturbed her so; she was only sure he did. She shouldn't hire him. She felt that instinctively. And yet he was so perfect for the job. She nodded her answer to him, not speaking, and his grin widened.

"That makes us even," he said softly. "I'd hire you, too."

"For what?" she asked without thinking.

He shrugged. "For anything at all." He raised an eyebrow. "How are you at shoeing horses? That's the only opening I've got right now."

Despite herself, she felt a smile creeping up on her. "Shoeing horses? I've never been closer to a horse than on a television screen."

He nodded sadly. "You're no horsewoman and I'm no model. I guess some things just aren't meant to be."

He started to turn away, and she touched his arm, pressing her card on him. "Just in case you change your mind," she said.

He took it, slipped it into his pocket, put a finger to his forehead as though he had a hat on and was saluting her, then turned toward the directory, his forefinger sliding down the list of occupants. He'd quite effectively dismissed her, and yet she found herself still standing behind him watching, unable to pull away. His finger stopped at the office number of an accounting firm, but she hardly noticed. She was too busy examining him and wondering why she'd ever hesitated about hiring him for the job. He was so perfect for the Caron Man. She could really see it now. Jeri was absolutely right.

He turned and saw her there, gave her a quizzical smile and started off down the hall.

"You'll keep us in mind?" she called after him.

He nodded without looking at her again, and Marlo slowly moved away. He wouldn't be back. She could tell. He had no interest in a modeling career. He had horses to shoe.

"Well?" Jeri was at the door of the office, standing on tiptoe as usual.

"Forget it," Marlo told her. "He's not going to do it."

Jeri flung herself into a chair. "Then we're doomed," she moaned.

Marlo bit her lip, straightened her shoulders and sat on the corner of the desk where Cal James had sat only a few minutes before. "Don't be silly, Jeri," she said, a bit more sharply than was probably necessary. "We're right back where we were an hour ago. There are still two more casting agencies ready to send us hordes of men to cull. Give them a call and have them send over all their prospects—" she glanced at the silver watch on her wrist "—first thing Monday morning. We'll find someone even better than that cowboy. You just wait and see."

Jeri's eyes were huge and doleful, and for once she was totally serious. "Don't you get it, Marlo?" she asked quietly. "He wasn't a model. He was the real thing. We'll never find a man like that from a casting agency."

Marlo knew that as well as Jeri did. "Well, what do you want me to do?" she asked in exasperation. "Go scout a rodeo? Hang out at the local Western bar?"

Jeri shook her head slowly. "No. I want you to sign Cal James."

The two women stared at each other for a long, long moment. Finally Marlo spoke. "Go call the agencies," she said evenly. "I've got to prepare for a meeting with Mr. Grayson."

Jeri left the office for her own desk with none of the usual spring in her step. Marlo watched her go, sighed and turned to her own work. A meeting with Mr. Grayson was a serious matter, especially when one was teetering on the edge of being fired.

Fired. How melodramatic that sounded. Would he really do that to her? Probably not. It would be much more his style to make things so unpleasant she'd quit on her own. She leaned back in her chair and stared at the ceiling. Yes, that's what he would do. He'd let her know in lots of little ways that he was disappointed in her. Why did that hurt so badly? She wasn't sure, but she knew she had to stop thinking along these lines or she'd end up going into the meeting with red eyes—and that would be the kiss of death. He didn't like signs of weakness.

She closed her eyes, took a deep breath, blotting out all thoughts of uncertainty and failure. She needed all her wits about her, just in case Mr. Grayson tried any fancy footwork. He wanted a progress report, and she was going to have to give him one. She pulled out the thumbnails—tiny pictures the art department had drawn to show her ideas for the ad campaign—and put them together with other documentation she wanted to have along. The more papers she could stick under his nose, the more secure she'd feel. If only she had the model lined up, she'd be ready for the comprehensives and . . .

Unbidden, a picture of the cowboy drifted into her mind. Jeri had been so right. He was a composite of every cowboy hero in the Western movies she used to see on television when she was a child. He had shoulders that looked as though they carried the weight of the sun on their span every day, eyes that saw beyond the horizon right into the dastardly heart of any bad guy who might cross his path, a tilt to his head that suggested he was listening to the distant sound of a coyote howling on a far mesa. He was good old-fashioned courage and strength, with an uncomplicated moral code that said he knew best and would act upon it. Where was she ever going to find another like him?

2

"WATCH OUT," Phillipa, Art Grayson's secretary, warned as Marlo entered the lavishly furnished reception area. "He's in a lousy mood."

That makes two of us, Marlo thought, but she smiled and said, "Mr. Grayson in a bad mood? I've never heard of such a thing."

Art Grayson was an operator, a smoothy who could charm the warts off a toad. Marlo ought to know. He'd charmed her right out of her job with Media Masters in Chicago and into his large agency, which occupied three floors of the huge TransUniversal Building in Los Angeles. The fact that he'd come to regret it had nothing to do with his skill at captivating people with flattery and humor.

"Well, you've heard of it now." Phillipa was a pleasingly plump, matronly lady, one of the few in the agency besides Jeri who'd been kind to Marlo since she arrived to work there six months before. The rumor was that Art Grayson had installed Phillipa after a succession of secretaries whose skills hadn't run to typing and answering phones.

"He hired her out of pure exhaustion," Jeri had told Marlo. "He was calling them in for dictation on the hour, but no letters ever went out. Even he couldn't handle quite that much temptation. So he got Phillipa, and now we can all depend upon at least one person at the top who knows what's going on."

And Phillipa did. Though she came across as a warm, motherly creature, she had a mind as sharp as a razor and kept the whole operation humming along. Marlo liked her a lot, and Phillipa returned the affection.

"He's hopping mad," Phillipa went on, wiggling her eyebrows significantly. "The Wormly people turned down the latest proposal on their new line of dog food and are talking of taking their business elsewhere. Heads, it seems, are going to roll." From her expression one might almost think she relished the idea. "Just take it from me. Mr. Grayson needs careful handling this afternoon."

Marlo smiled. "I'll remember that. Shall I go on in?"

Phillipa escorted her into the gloomy, cherry-wood paneled office, winked at her and closed the door. Marlo walked toward the desk, not noticing for a second that Art Grayson wasn't sitting behind it, but was off to the side, staring out the steel-blinded window at the smoggy Los Angeles sky.

"Mr. Grayson?" she asked tentatively.

He didn't turn to face her, nor did he answer.

"Art?" She walked toward him. "Is something wrong?"

Just before she reached him, his shoulders seemed to straighten and he whirled. "Sit down, Marlo," he barked. "I want to talk to you."

She retreated quickly, her papers clutched to her chest. Was this it, then? Had he had enough of her mistakes? Was this the end? Her heart hammered painfully in her chest, but she held her head high. Things had gone wrong ever since she'd arrived at Grayson's agency, but there were explanations for every failure. She knew it had been bad luck rather than incompetence that had hampered her work. She only wished there was a way to let him know it without sounding like a whiner.

She slipped into the chair facing the huge gleaming desk, and he threw himself down into his chair, sinking low, staring at her broodingly. He was a handsome man in his mid-forties, tall and broad shouldered, his dark hair streaked attractively with silver. It was hardly surprising that he had a reputation. Women tended to swoon as he passed, and he couldn't really be blamed for taking advantage of his good fortune. Marlo didn't fault him for it at all. She only faulted those in the agency who took it for granted that swooning was what had gotten her the job she held.

She'd met Grayson in Chicago. He'd been impressed with her work on an ad campaign for a chain of children's stores, and he wasted no time in offering her a job with his firm. She'd taken it gladly, ready for a change after five years with Media Masters. It was only after she'd moved West that she realized people assumed she'd come to do other things than work.

"I'll bet you're living at the Waikiki Palms Apartments on Beverly, aren't you?" the clerk in Personnel had said with a giggle when she first arrived to fill out her tax and employment forms.

"How did you know?" Marlo had asked with a naive smile.

The woman gave her an "oh, come on now" sort of look. "That's where Mr. Grayson puts all his...friends," she'd said coyly.

It was true. Art Grayson had found the apartment for her. But Marlo let the incident pass, thinking it only a coincidence. Living space was at a premium in Southern California, and once one found a place to stay, one kept it. The thought of having an affair with Art Grayson held no appeal at all for her, and though he'd taken her out to dinner in Chicago, he'd never made a pass. Her conscience was totally clear. She liked the man. Despite his gruff exterior and flashy reputation she often had the feeling that he really cared about people on a human level. He just didn't know how to show it very well.

She only wished more of her co-workers in the agency were as well-meaning. She'd gone to the first staff meetings and lunches with an open mind and a ready smile. She'd never had any problem making friends before. It was bewildering to be met with stony stares and enigmatic, sarcastic remarks. She wasn't sure at first if it were her, or if she'd fallen in with a group of nasty people. Not until Art assigned Jeri to her did she find out what was bothering everyone.

"They think you got this job by sleeping with the boss." Jeri pulled no punches.

"But I never..." Marlo didn't know whether to laugh or cry.

"I know that now," Jeri told her blithely. "But I thought the same thing until I transferred in here. You see, two copywriters in the art department—Ted Hanford and Jill Nettles—thought they had the inside track on this job. They were fighting tooth and nail over it. Blood was flowing down the halls, everyone was betting on who would survive. And then, all of a sudden, you walk in and settle down like Little Miss Muffet." Jeri grinned as though the picture she'd painted delighted her. "Naturally, everyone assumed you got the job in the bedroom."

Naturally. Marlo had been appalled, but had also been sure she'd prove her worth so quickly they'd all have to eat crow. And then everything began to go wrong. Now she knew all the other employees of Grayson's felt vindicated in their belief in her unworthiness. She could just hear the comments as they passed her office. "See? I told you she couldn't cut it. When he gets tired of her, she'll be out on her ear."

It made her seethe with anger and resentment—and embarrassment. She wanted to prove them wrong so badly. But nothing seemed to go right for her. Now she had such a good idea for the Caron ads, and that cowboy wouldn't cooperate. And from the look on Art Grayson's face, he might be ready to yank her from the project, anyway.

"Are you a fighter, Marlo?" he asked at last, leaning forward and thrusting his chin toward her.

Marlo opened her mouth to reply, then closed it again. What on earth was the man leading up to? "I— I consider myself something of a fighter."

He nodded slowly, still staring at her, his hazel eyes piercing. "Good." He grimaced and settled back into his chair, turning it sideways so that he could look out at the city again. "No matter what they say, it's a sink-or-swim world out there. You've got to fight to make it. I had to fight to make this agency what it is."

Marlo moved uncomfortably in her chair, not sure if this was a pep talk meant to bolster her spirits, or something else. "I'm sure you did," she began, but he didn't seem interested in conversation.

"When I was a kid," he went on, gripping the armrests of his chair, "I was a puny little guy. I was always getting beat up, shoved around." He spun the chair around and stared at her again. "I wanted to get bigger, so I ate everything I could get my hands on. But all that did was make me fat, and then they used me for a human punching bag."

Marlo reached out with her hand, wanting to comfort the little boy he'd been, but not sure how, or why he was telling her this. Her hand dropped to the desk, and he went on, not noticing her gesture.

"Swimmers were big and strong. I tried to get on the swim team, but they didn't want me. The coach said I was too small, plus I had asthma. They wouldn't allow me in the pool." He leaned forward again. "So I went down to the river, and I swam and swam every day after school, choking on the dirty water, knocking into sticks and garbage, but working and working at it, even into November. And when I went back to the Y and told them I could beat any of them in the hundred-yard freestyle, they laughed. But I beat them all. And they had to let me on the team." He sat back, a satisfied smile on his face. "I'm a fighter, Marlo. That's how I got where I am today, by working harder than anyone else." He leaned forward, staring hard into her eyes, as though to impress his point on her by sheer willpower. "And that's what you have to do."

She nodded, eyes wide. She felt like a prize-fighter being psyched up for the big bout. He must really believe she was floundering if he thought she needed this. If only she could show him . . . "Would you like to see the plans for the Caron account?" she asked tentatively.

He glanced down at her folders as though surprised she'd brought up the subject. "Not now." He rose, towering over her. Suddenly she was reminded of her father, and she looked quickly down at her hands, knotted together in her lap. "Show me later. I've got things to think about right now." He came around the desk and stopped by her chair, leaned down and gave her a fatherly pat. "I know you can do it, Marlo," he said heartily. "I've got faith in you."

She rose a bit shakily, knowing she was being dismissed. Tears were stinging behind her eyes, and she wanted to get out of the office before he noticed. "Thank you, Mr. Grayson," she managed to sputter.

"Art. Call me Art." He took her hand in his and shook it, beaming at her with obvious affection. "I don't know why I have to tell you that every time I talk to you."

The next thing she knew she was being ushered out the door of his office. She blinked as though coming into sunlight from a dark cave. She appreciated Mr. Grayson's faith, but she couldn't help but wonder if it had much staying power. She was going to have to do something to justify it, and fast. After all, how many of these little pep talks could she take?

"How did it go?" Phillipa wanted to know as she left.

"Weird," Marlo told her softly, shaking her head. "Not bad, but very weird."

AND THAT WORD just about summed up her day, she decided as she drove home through the congestion on Wilshire Boulevard. She pulled into the parking garage and ran up to her second-story apartment, changing quickly into her swimsuit. Art's talk about the swim team had reminded her that she'd once gained a lot of peace and satisfaction from swimming laps on hot afternoons. Maybe a strenuous workout would help take the weirdness out of her day.

She walked out onto the patio a little self-consciously. She'd never used the swimming pool in the middle of the courtyard that separated the two long buildings, and she was very much aware of how white her legs looked. She tried to carry her towel strategically placed to cover as much of her revealed skin as possible.

A small group of men were wading in the shallow end of the pool, each with a drink in a plastic cup. Two young women in skimpy suits lay on chaise longues very near them, and there was a lot of teasing going back and forth. Marlo threw the group a quick smile as she passed, heading for the deep end.

She felt them go silent as they watched her, but she tried not to pay any attention. She hadn't made an effort to meet her neighbors, and she'd been rebuffed so many times at work that she'd given up hope of finding friends in her new home. She just tried to avoid making enemies.

Throwing her towel down on a chair, she slipped out of her sandals and walked toward the sparkling blue water. It looked cool and inviting, and she felt no hesitation in diving into its silvery depths. The refreshing water rushed around her, tiny shining bubbles flying away behind her as she swam. She reveled in the stretch of her body, the caressing slide of the water as she slipped through it. She'd forgotten how good it was to swim like this.

She swam past the group at the end of the pool, then back to the other end. She lost count of how many times she went the length, but when she finally stopped, she made sure to do so at the deep end, holding onto the side and working to get back the breath she'd lost. She felt gloriously alive and healthy.

She turned and looked at the person beside her in the water. One of the men from the laughing group had detached himself from the others and come down to her end of the pool. Marlo noted that he looked barely old enough to have graduated from college. She glanced down the pool and saw that the others had gone on with their teasing and were paying no attention.

"Hello," she said, making her smile friendly but noncommittal.

"I'm Peter Moore," he said, grinning with happy interest. His big brown eyes were puppy-dog eager.

"I'm Marlo Santee," she returned, liking the look of him in spite of herself. His slender shoulders were sunburned, sticking out of the water like a boy's. His face was slightly freckled, his reddish-brown hair cut short at the sides and long on top in the modern style.

"Marlo. That's pretty." He took a deep breath, frowned as though concentrating, then licked his lower lip and spoke again.

"Okay," he said, holding a finger up in front of her face. "Here goes. Listen closely." He drew back his head, narrowed his eyes and recited quickly, "Basketball, Beethoven, Bruce Springsteen, sushi, Scorpios, Ferraris, Brie, Johannesberg Riesling, making love in a hot tub, sailboarding, knee socks and penny Loafers, long black hair, walking on the beach under a full moon and black lacy nightgowns."

He finally stopped, and she wasn't sure if he was finished or only getting his second wind. But she laughed anyway. "What was that?" she asked.

"It's the latest thing," he told her cheerfully. "It's called Instant Intimacy. You now know all the things I like. You tell me the same things about you, and we'll already know each other as well as though we'd been dating for weeks."

The thought of the two of them dating was even more amusing. "Beethoven and Bruce Springsteen, huh?" She was laughing again. "I'll bet you look really cute in those lacy nightgowns."

To her amazement he flushed. "Not for me, of course," he told her quite seriously. "On a woman."

"Oh, of course." She nodded wisely. He was so very young. "What do you do, Peter?"

"I'm a junior executive at Ployton Electronics," he revealed. "Now you tell me all about yourself."

She grinned. "I'm twenty-eight years old," she told him simply. "That's all you really need to know about me."

He didn't bat an eye. "I love experienced women," he said.

Experienced women. The poor boy! She almost choked, but managed to keep her humor in hand. She probably had less experience than the average sixteen-year-old, if the rumors she'd heard about today's teenagers were even half true. Not that she'd lived the life of a recluse. She'd had her share of dates in high school and again in college. But since then work had been the most important thing in her life. She had something to prove, and though she'd worked very hard, she still hadn't proved it.

In the meantime here was this young man, obviously smitten with her for the moment. How best to dissuade him without hurting his feelings? The first thing that came to mind was to tell him, "I don't love inexperienced men." But she had a feeling that would only bring forth a catalog of his past experiences, perhaps with references attached, and she didn't think she was ready for that.

"I hope you find one, then," she murmured with a smile, reaching for the chrome ladder that would take her out of the pool. But just as her hand connected with the metal, her eyes focused on the far side of the pool, and suddenly she was sinking back into the water, trying to hide.

A man was coming out of a ground-floor apartment not fifty feet away. He was tall and broad shouldered, wearing jeans and cowboy boots, and this time a Stetson was perched on his head. Could it be Cal James? Her first thought was, *Don't let him see me in this bathing suit!* But he didn't look toward the pool at all. He was talking to someone inside the apartment.

"Do you like to go dancing?" The voice came from behind. Peter hadn't given up.

She shook her head, not looking back, and he began babbling about some dance club in Marina Del Rey. But she paid no attention. Her gaze was full of the cowboy.

Then his companion came out of the apartment, and her heart did an inexplicable flip in her chest before tumbling to her feet. Of course it was a woman. And, also of course, she was a striking blond beauty. Marlo watched as the cowboy curled an arm around her bare shoulders, drawing her close, and began to escort her through the courtyard to the street. Then he turned and she saw his face plainly. It was as long and friendly as a Saint Bernard's, and it wasn't Cal James's.

And here she was, lying low in the water with just her eyes showing, coming up to get a breath only when it was absolutely necessary.

"Like a hippopotamus in a mud hole," she said disgustedly later on when she was back in her own apartment and analyzing what had happened. It had certainly not been her finest hour. Here she'd thought the man she'd wanted—no, make that needed—desperately to bring success to her ad campaign was walking right past her nose. And she hadn't peeped because she was so concerned with his not seeing her in a swimsuit. It was ridiculous, and she was thoroughly angry with herself.

She'd watched until the cowboy and the blonde disappeared through the breezeway between the buildings. Then she'd shaken off Peter's heavy-handed attempts to sweep her off her feet, pulled herself out of the pool, grabbed her towel and sandals and run upstairs into her apartment.

After a stinging shower she took a TV dinner out of the freezer and prepared for another lonely evening. What would she do if she ever did get another chance at Cal James? She would remind him of her offer. "It could start a whole new career for you," she would say. "The money can be quite good." And she would let him know in no uncertain terms that she wanted him for the ad, wanted him very badly.

But it was too late now. The odds were good that she would never see him again. If only that had been him by the pool . . .

Then she remembered the sick lurch in the general vicinity of her stomach when she'd thought she was seeing Cal James put his arm around the pretty blonde. Her reaction had been a little silly, hadn't it? Good-looking men usually came with attractive women attached. The world worked that way. Two by two. Man and woman. Partners. The fact that she'd chosen another way for herself didn't mean everyone else should do the same. Of course he was attached, perhaps even married. It stood to reason.

It was nothing to her, after all. The man had kissed her, true, but only as a joke. Still, her stomach churned and she looked down at her dinner in disgust, pushing it across the little table. If she was getting this silly over a joke kiss, maybe she'd been without male companionship for a bit too long. She got up and walked to the full-length mirror at the end of her hallway, pulling off her robe and staring critically at her figure.

Not bad. But it could use a little work. Without giving herself time to think of why she might be suddenly so concerned, she went to the VCR, put in an exercise tape and began doing aerobics with determined energy. Never again was she going to be caught flat-footed because she didn't want someone to see her in a bathing suit.

By Sunday night she felt like a shipwreck survivor—one who'd had to tread water for a long, long time. She'd spent the entire weekend bouncing and stretching to lively music, swimming laps in the pool and lying in the sun, turning every fifteen minutes to maintain an even tan. Well, it had begun as a tan. By Sunday evening it was a sunburn. Probably the only thing that had kept her from sunstroke was Peter's presence. He was always hovering around, offering to get her drinks or rub on suntan lotion. Finally he drove her back into her apartment for a little peace.

JERI DID A DOUBLE TAKE when Marlo walked into the office Monday morning. She held up her hands as though to shield herself from the light. "Wow. Is this a publicity gimmick or what? You look like a neon sign."

"Thank you very much for that boost to my already shriveled self-image," Marlo answered with a touch of sardonic humor. "How are we coming on finding the Caron Man? Did you call the casting agencies?"

She nodded. "Twenty-four gorgeous specimens, coming right up, each guaranteed to be the man of your dreams."

Marlo rolled her eyes. "I'll believe that when I see it."

Jeri giggled. "And see it you will, beginning at ten o'clock when the first batch of little cuties is due to arrive." She sighed happily. "I always love these cattle calls."

Marlo mumbled something unintelligible and retreated into her office. She didn't love them at all. She had a feeling of doom about the whole project. She knew they weren't going to find anyone like Cal James. She'd left the house without her usual morning coffee, her sunburn hurt and her headache was back. Perhaps she was becoming allergic to Grayson's Advertising Agency.

The telephone rang insistently. It was Mr. Caron, wanting to know when she would be ready with the comprehensives. She put him off as tactfully as she could, promising him a presentation date and hoping she could make it. She wished she'd become a librarian instead of going into advertising. The thought of cool, dark halls filled with books and silence seemed awfully inviting.

Beginning right at ten o'clock the men began to stream through the office. Tall ones, short ones, dark ones, blond ones—they all blurred into a masculine mush before Marlo's glazed eyes. Not one of them had the cool arrogance, the easy mastery of Cal James. Not one of them looked as if he'd know what to do if a damsel in distress shrieked, or even if the nearest horse let out a snort. They were handsome, pleasant, attractive men, but they weren't the Caron Man that Marlo had carried around in her head and heart for weeks now. No one could fill that part but Cal James.

"It's no use, is it?" Jeri said as the last of them filed out the door.

"Never say die," Marlo mumbled, but her heart wasn't in it.

The door opened again and a round, handsome face with huge, doleful brown eyes gazed in at them. It was Ted Hanford, one of the copywriters who thought he should have Marlo's job.

"Hello, Ted." Marlo managed to summon a smile. "What can I do for you?"

He smiled back and entered the office. "Better to ask what I can do for you," he said enigmatically. "I understand you're having some trouble on the Caron account."

Wary prickles beat a path down Marlo's spine. "Now, Ted, whatever gave you that idea?" she asked, hoping she sounded serene, but doubting she'd quite pulled it off.

Ted shrugged his shoulders. "Oh, I don't know. Perhaps it was the panic lines around your pretty mouth." His grin was not so much malicious as satisfied. "Or the scent of desperation in the air." He glanced down at Jeri, who was seething. "Or the fevered brow of your assistant."

"I'll show you fever!" Jeri sputtered, lurching out of her chair, but Marlo stopped her with a restraining hand.

"We appreciate your concern, Ted," she said dryly, "but everything's under control."

He raised a disbelieving eyebrow. "No doubt." He turned to go. "Remember, it always gets darkest just before it goes absolutely pitch-black." He pulled open the door and looked back at them, his grin wide and happy. "Let me know if I can provide comfort in my own small way." And he was gone.

"I'll kill him," Jeri threatened, bouncing up and down. "Just bring him back in here, and I'll tear him limb from limb!"

Marlo didn't bother to respond to Jeri's overreaction, nor did she question it. Jeri always seemed to lose her composure around Ted. Marlo had never discovered the reason, and over time she'd come to accept it as the norm.

She put a hand to her head, trying to stop the thundering headache. Something had to be done, something a little more helpful than beating up the enemies. "Remember what we said about visiting a rodeo..." she began, but Jeri was a step ahead of her.

"I've already tried that. There is no rodeo in town and won't be for two months. The closest this month is in Phoenix or in Denver."

Marlo tried to smile. "How would you like a week's vacation in sunny Arizona?"

Jeri hesitated. "If it comes to that . . ."

"It has come to that. The Caron people will be expecting comprehensives and a thorough presentation the beginning of next week. We have to come up with something. It's either that or change the entire thrust of the campaign."

Jeri shrugged. "Just tell me what you want, boss. I'll do what I can."

Marlo looked at her and suddenly her anxiety dissolved in a warm smile. What would she do without this loyal person at her side? "Thanks, Jeri," she said, her voice a little rough with emotion. "I'd like you to fly out to Phoenix tomorrow. If you see anything good, I'll come join you on Thursday."

Jeri's grin was mischievous. "Will my per diem cover cowboy clothes?" she asked. "I'll want to fit in with the cowpunchers at the rodeo."

"You treat yourself to whatever you think you can get by Finance, and if they won't okay something, I'll pay for it."

But her confidence faded as she shut the door on Jeri's retreating figure. She really didn't have much hope that Jeri would find what they wanted, even at a rodeo. The qualities they were looking for were old-fashioned, had just about died out with the twentieth century. The man who possessed them would have to be very special indeed, and the only one who'd come close was Cal James. Would she ever have another chance to win him over?

Before the day ended, that chance presented itself. Marlo was driving home in the late evening traffic. She was about three blocks from home when there he was, standing before the open hood of an old Mustang convertible, which was sitting disabled at the side of the road.

3

MARLO DROVE around the block once to make sure it was really him and then again to make sure no one was with him. But he was all alone, leaning over the engine, poking at something she couldn't see. On the third pass she pulled over and parked in front of him. He didn't look up, and she sat for a moment, just watching him. She wished she knew the magic words that would make him take the job she offered. She was nervous, and she was sure it was because of the importance of what she was about to do. That was all. Wasn't it?

"Hi," she called, getting out of her car at last, slamming her door with a thunk to give herself courage. "Having trouble?"

He barely glanced her way, no sign of recognition on his tan face. "Just a little fuel pump problem," he said offhandedly. "I've already called the auto club."

She realized she looked different from the Friday before. Then she'd worn her hair down and flowing, but had dressed in her usual business suit. Today she'd tied her black hair away from her face and had worn a light cotton sundress, hoping to keep as much air as possible between her sunburned skin and fabric.

"Is there anything I can do?" she asked, coming up beside him.

"No, not really." He began to wipe his hands on a cloth he'd pulled from his pocket. "Thanks anyway."

She had the distinct feeling she'd heard that tone before and realized with a start that it was the one she'd used when trying to get rid of Peter over the weekend. Her first instinct was to slink off and leave Cal alone, if that was what he wanted. But then she toughened herself. She was a woman with a purpose. This time she wasn't going to let him get away.

"At least I can keep you company until the tow truck comes," she said bravely.

He paused at that, straightening to his full height, and when he really looked at her, his face changed. "Say, aren't you the lady who was going to make me a star?" he asked, beginning a lazy grin.

She found herself grinning back. The warmth in his eyes was infectious. "That's me," she answered. "Ready to give it a try?"

He didn't answer right away. He looked her up and down, and she felt herself sizzle slightly where his gaze lingered. But it was a nice feeling. She usually hated it when men were so obvious, but something about the way he did it made her feel pretty instead of violated.

He chuckled softly as he leaned back against his car. "I'm sure you've found yourself a proper Western man by now."

She took in his profile, imagining a shot of that jagged silhouette against a clear blue sky. What an ad that would make! "As a matter of fact, we haven't," she told him. "I've just spent the day interviewing man after man, twenty-four in all, none of whom came anywhere near the mark."

"You're kidding. What was wrong with them?"

She swallowed hard, hoping he didn't hear her heart pounding. "None of them was you," she forced out.

His eyes narrowed. "Still perfect, am I?" he asked quietly.

She nodded. "You're exactly what we need. No one else comes close."

He stared into her eyes, not a trace of humor evident. "Maybe you ought to change your priorities," he suggested.

She shook her head, capturing him with her own wide eyes. "It's too late," she said evenly. "Now that I've seen you, I don't want anyone else." Good grief, it sounded as though she was in love with him, but how else could she put it? She was fiercely determined to get him if she could, no matter what she had to do.

To her surprise his gaze hardened until he looked almost angry. "Then you're in trouble, lady," he said slowly, his voice sharp as ground glass. "Because I'm not interested."

She'd been expecting more humor, not the defense he was erecting. "You haven't let me tell you anything about the job," she said quickly, hoping to get in as much information as possible before he cut her off. "The hours will be sporadic and long on the days we shoot, but you'll have a lot of time off in between assignments. We'll require a six-month contract with option to renew for another six months, and if we go for the extension, there will be public appearances—"

"Not interested."

"The money is bound to tempt you," she hurried on. She named a figure way above any she'd ever paid before, knowing she was going to have a hard time coming up with that much for a model with no experience, but saying anything to make him listen.

She searched his expression to see what he thought of that amount and found him shaking his head. "Now what would I do with all that money?" he asked as though exasperated.

"I don't know. Buy a new car, maybe." Surely he would like something newer.

"A new car?" He sounded incredulous. "You mean, get rid of this old clunker, huh?" Suddenly, as though against his better judgment, he was laughing, but that was better than the anger.

She glanced at his face, relieved to see the harshness gone. "If you want to keep it, go ahead. Use the money for something else. Maybe you'd like a new horse."

"A new horse." He burst out laughing again, and just as he did, the tow truck pulled up behind his wounded car. "A new horse." He was still laughing and shaking his head when the mechanic came up. "Hi, there," Cal greeted him. "The lady thinks I ought to get rid of this old jalopy and get myself something worthwhile, like a brand-new LTD maybe, or a Corolla. What do you think?"

The mechanic didn't bat an eye. "You ever want to sell this little gem, buddy, you give me a call." He pulled out a card and stuck it in Cal's hand. "Meanwhile, I'll get her hooked up for the trip back to the shop."

Marlo gritted her teeth. So maybe the car was some sort of antique. How was she to know? That wasn't the point. "Wait," she said, catching hold of Cal's arm before he could go with the mechanic. "I need you. I'm desperate. I'll . . ." She shrugged helplessly, beseeching him with her eyes. "Name your price."

The mechanic, who'd heard every word, let out a low whistle. "Some guys have all the luck," he muttered as he walked behind the car to hook the chains together.

Marlo flushed, but she didn't let go. "I mean it," she said fiercely. "Listen, let me take you to dinner so we can talk about it."

He held her gaze for a long moment. "No," he said at last. "There'd be no purpose to that. I'm not going to do the job, and I won't waste your time."

She opened her mouth to plead, but nothing came out. He began to pry her fingers from his arm, just as he'd done to Jeri's a few days before.

"You go on back to your swanky office, lady," he said gently. "You'll be better off without me."

He turned away and she watched him walk over to help the mechanic. She stood still for a few moments, heedless of the rush-hour traffic that sped by just a few feet away. He didn't look up again, and finally she walked to her car.

She got in and sat in the driver's seat, feeling drained and desolate, as though she'd lost something important to her. He wasn't going to do it. The Caron ads were going to be a flop. She would lose her job, her self-respect, everything.

But it was more than that, and she knew it. She felt as though she'd lost a lover, as though the man in her life had just walked out. "You're crazy," she whispered to herself, leaning over the steering wheel. "You're acting like a crazy person." But she couldn't help it. She was shaking so badly she didn't dare try to drive.

He wasn't going to do the ads. Somehow, deep down, she'd thought he would. A tiny part of her had been sure she'd find him again, and that he would do them.

What an idiot she was to think he was something special. What had he ever done to make her think that, anyway? It was only her own overactive imagination that had built him up in her mind. She might as well come back down to earth.

She wasn't sure how long she sat there, but suddenly Cal was at her window, leaning way down so that he could talk to her. "Are you trying to put me on a guilt trip, lady?" he asked, his eyes smiling.

She shook her head, but the lump in her throat wouldn't let her talk.

"Oh, hell," he said. "Listen, this Caron Man—you want a Western type to play him, right?"

She nodded.

"Well, I know where there are hordes of cowboys, lots of them tougher than I am. You want to go take a look?"

She wasn't sure what he was driving at, but she nodded, eyes shining.

His hand slapped the side of her car. "Then unlock the passenger's door and let me in," he said, walking around the car. She did so and he folded his long form into her compact car.

Feeling a little bit triumphant, a little bit wary, she asked, "What about your car?"

"The garage will keep it until tomorrow," he told her. "In the meantime I'm counting on you for my transportation. Okay?"

There was a huge bubble of happiness about to burst in her chest; she was chagrined that it should be so, but she couldn't help it. "Absolutely," she said, starting the engine. "How do we get to this cowboy haven?"

"Well, you can bet it's not on Wilshire." He laughed. "Better take the freeway. We're going toward the Valley."

She was still shaking, but now it was a tremble of delight. She smiled to herself, not sure if her happiness was based on his mere presence, or if she was just glad to have a further opportunity to talk him into doing the ads. No matter. She was going to enjoy herself.

Cal seemed to have forgotten his momentary anger. As they sped along, he kept up a running commentary, amusing her with anecdotes and jokes about the places they passed. When they pulled up in front of the Cherokee Waters, Marlo had lost all her nervousness and was feeling like herself again.

"What is this place?" she asked, peering at the weathered building.

"It's kind of a country steak house with music," he told her. "I think you're going to like it."

The music drifted out across the parking lot. Cal draped an arm around her shoulders to lead her to the restaurant.

"Ouch!" She pulled back sharply. "Sunburn," she explained.

"So that's it," he replied. "And here all this time I thought you were just blushing." He looked her over with a practiced eye. "What have you been doing?"

"Just sitting out by the pool at my apartment."

"I won't touch you again." He grinned. "Unless you ask me to, of course," he teased.

She looked away, embarrassed and not able to think of a good reply. "Shall we go in?"

The music was very loud inside. The room was wide and dark, with a low ceiling and long wooden tables stretching out from the stage like spokes on a wheel. Patrons were seated along the tables, some drinking beer, some eating. Only a few seemed to be paying any attention to the young woman wailing country sorrow into the microphone.

"Hello, Martin," Cal said to the man at the door. "It's been a long time."

"Cal!" The manager seemed glad to see him, beaming and shaking his hand with enthusiasm. "Rosie, get over here!" he called to a tall, heavyset woman dressed in red. "It's Cal."

"Cal James!" The woman threw her arms around him and hugged with all her might. "Where have you been? We haven't seen you in so long. We thought you'd moved or something."

"I wouldn't leave without telling you, Rosie." Cal planted a loud kiss on her rouged cheek. "I've brought someone with me."

They turned to stare at Marlo, and she felt like a specimen under glass. "A girl?" they asked simultaneously, as though he'd brought in something from another planet.

"A woman," he corrected jovially. "Marlo, meet Martin and Rose Perez. They run this place together."

"Pleased to meet you," said Rosie, and Martin grunted as he extended his hand. But Marlo could tell they both had their doubts. What was it about her that put them off? She wasn't sure, but she could see the coolness shadow their eyes when they turned from Cal to her.

"Come on, honey." Rosie returned to her former warmth when she spoke to Cal. "I'll find you the best seat in the house."

Cal's eyes were twinkling wickedly. "We need some-place that's good for cowboy watching," he said with a straight face.

"What?" Rosie came up short, black eyes wide.

Cal sighed and gestured with his hand. "It's Marlo. She's looking for another man, someone to take my place, so we want to sit where the pickings are good."

Marlo's mouth dropped with indignation as Rosie threw her a disdainful glance. "I don't know, Cal," the large lady muttered as she led them to a section of tables near the stage. "You always pick them, don't you?"

"I do, don't I?" he answered cheerfully, surveying the room and waving back at a few people who saluted him. "But don't you worry about me, Rosie. You know what they say. Once bitten, twice shy."

Rosie scowled at Marlo. "Some women just don't know gold from river-bottom mud," she muttered darkly. "Sometimes I think you're one of those what-chacallems—masochists." She shook her head. "I'll get you two a couple of beers and then be back to take your order."

Marlo sat beside Cal and looked around the room. The lights were dim, but she could see there was a good crowd. Cal leaned close.

"Well, what do you think?" he asked, nodding at a large man passing their table.

She gave him a mock glare. Didn't he understand yet that she wasn't interested in anyone but him? "Too tall," she said.

He frowned. "I can tell you're not going to be a pushover, but we've got enough bolo ties and cowboy boots in this place to stock a rodeo. We'll find some-thing."

She smiled. "I'm sending Jeri to a rodeo in Phoenix tomorrow. Do you think she'll have any luck?"

"All the way to Phoenix?" He stared at her. "You people are serious about this, aren't you?"

"Absolutely," she replied.

His eyes captured hers for a long moment, then he shook his head. "I'm going to go wash up," he said gruffly, pushing back his chair and holding up hands still stained from his work on the car. "Be right back."

She watched him go, his every movement a fluid act of grace, and remembered how she'd asked him to walk for her. A smile tilted her mouth at the thought.

"You two been going together long?" Rosie asked grumpily as she put down the glasses and poured out two bottles of beer.

"No," Marlo began, "actually—"

"I just want to have my say, and then I'll keep my mouth shut," Rosie said, hands on her hips. "Cal James is a good man. One of the best. His only fault is his choice of women." She said the word as though it left a bad taste in her mouth. "He's been raked over the coals enough for one lifetime. If another woman treats him that way, we—" she threw her arms open, implying that each and every one of her customers was a close personal friend of Cal's "—wouldn't like it." She frowned ferociously at Marlo.

"No, listen," Marlo implored. "We're just here on business, honest. This isn't a date."

Rosie looked skeptical. "Just treat him right," she said gruffly. "He deserves it." Then she turned and stalked away.

Marlo watched her go, not knowing whether to be offended or touched by Rosie's concern. But before she could decide, she saw Cal across the room, and inexplicably her pulse leaped and a series of shivers ran down her spine.

She looked down into her beer as he came back toward the table, shocked at the way she was responding to him and determined that he shouldn't know a thing about it. As he slid into his seat beside her, an older, gray-haired man came up to talk to him, and she took the opportunity to ponder the cowboy who'd set her senses out of kilter.

Rosie had implied that Cal had been hurt in the past, and hurt badly. Was that why a flickering melancholy seemed to dart behind the humor in his eyes? Was that why he sometimes seemed wary, reluctant?

"Too old?" he murmured close to her ear, and she realized she'd been staring after his friend, who was now heading back to his own table.

She nodded, searching Cal's face for a clue to his background. She liked what she saw. She'd liked almost everything about him from the first. How could any woman hurt a man like this?

"Don't worry," he said, mistaking her expression. "We'll find you a good cowboy, if it takes all night."

They ate steak and corn on the cob and barbecued beans and sourdough bread while visitor after visitor came to their table. It seemed what Rosie had implied was true: everyone in the place was a friend of Cal's.

The country singer was replaced by a bluegrass band, and Marlo found herself joining all the others, clapping her hands and stomping her feet along with the music.

"You like anybody in the band?" Cal asked, nodding toward the stage. "I guarantee any one of them would jump at the chance to model for you."

"Too skinny," she said, glancing at the bulge of Cal's biceps, clearly defined beneath the checkered material of his shirt.

He followed her glance and, to her amusement, seemed almost embarrassed. "I thought the camera added ten pounds," he mused.

"It does," she agreed. "But in all the wrong places."

The bluegrass band was replaced by a small string group that played slow, easy, melancholy songs from decades past. Rosie came and took away their plates.

"You two having a good time?" she asked, and as her eyes met Marlo's, they sharpened with warning.

"The food was terrific, as usual. And the music's great." Cal leaned back in his chair and sighed. "But we're having some trouble with the quality of men your place attracts, Rosie. They just don't seem to be good enough for Marlo. How am I going to find her a cowboy if I can't find her one here?"

Rosie was speechless, her broad face bewildered. Marlo smiled, hoping her look conveyed what she was thinking. *See? I told you we weren't dating.* And finally Rosie seemed to understand, if grudgingly.

"How about this guy coming up?" Cal whispered to Marlo at one point. "Take a look at those shoulders! His name's Bronc, and he could throw a Brahman bull if you gave him half a chance. How about him?"

"Hey, Cal." Bronc was big and handsome, with a smile that needed sunglasses to look at. "Where you been hiding out?" He glanced at Marlo. "Or need I ask?"

The man was attractive, but a little too slick. He flirted with Marlo while he backslapped Cal, and when he finally left, Marlo shook her head. "Not good enough," she told Cal.

He sighed. "I know it's hard to improve upon perfection, honey, but you've got to make a choice somewhere along the line."

"I did make one," she said without hesitation. "I chose you."

He was silent and she didn't dare turn to see why. "Can you dance?" he asked at last.

"Can I dance?" she repeated. "What a question! Why, do I look as though I might step on your feet?"

"No." He grinned. "I'm talking about your sunburn." He gestured toward her bare shoulders. "Is there anyplace I can hold you that won't hurt?"

Anywhere. The word almost slipped out before she caught it. Her heart began to beat a quickening rhythm in her chest. The thought of being held in his arms was stopping the breath in her throat. He could hold her anywhere. She'd ignore the pain.

"I—I wore a one-piece suit," she told him almost shyly. "The worst sunburn is on my shoulders and legs."

"Come on." He led her to the small dance floor. "Put your arms around my waist if it'll hurt to raise them higher," he said, taking her in his arms.

She did as he suggested, feeling a little awkward at first, but soon getting into the swing of the soft music. They started out leaning away from each other, smiling into each other's eyes, but gradually they pulled closer and closer together, and finally her body touched his hard form for the first time, and she had to close her eyes to hold back the shock of it.

She was falling and she knew it. There was still one tiny sane area of her mind screaming, "What are you doing? A cowboy, for Pete's sake! You, the stereotypical city girl, falling for a man who spends most of his time riding around on something with four legs? A man who wears denim and boots? Be serious!" But the rest of her wasn't listening.

Her cheek rested against his chest, and when his arms tightened around her, she blocked out the stinging of her crisp skin. She didn't want to do anything to make him stop. His body was hard and smooth and wonderful, like nothing she'd ever felt before. She was floating in a haze, aware only of the man in her arms, of her own responses.

Vaguely she realized the music had stopped and their feet were no longer moving. She felt his warm breath ruffle her hair and knew what would happen if she looked up. Slowly she raised her face. They were standing in the shadows at the far end of the room, but she could see the turmoil in his dark eyes. He was going to kiss her, but he was doing it reluctantly, like a man unable to resist, not like a man on the make. She parted her lips, waiting, and then his mouth covered hers, reaching hungrily, slightly uncontrolled.

She felt a tiny answering cry rising in her throat, but his kiss stilled it. The anger was there again, woven into the fabric of his caress. She felt it, but that only made her more eager to please, more eager to soothe and protect him. There was pain behind the anger, some wound that hadn't healed. She wanted to be the one to apply the salve that cured him. She reached up a hand to touch his cheek, and at the same time his embrace shifted, crunching her sunburned skin, and she gasped in pain.

He swore sharply, pulling away immediately. She wasn't sure if the curse was for her agony or for his own. "I'm sorry," he mumbled, taking her hand to lead her back to their table. "I wasn't planning to be such an idiot."

She followed him quietly, wishing she knew what she could say to bring back the lighthearted tone they'd had before. He glanced at his watch as they sat down. "It's getting late," he said shortly. "I'd better get you home."

She glanced at him sideways and toyed with her drink. "Haven't you got that backward?" she asked. "I'm the one who drove."

He sat back as though thunderstruck. "That's right! How am I going to get home?"

"I'll take you, of course. I said I'd be your transportation."

He reached for her hand. "You don't know where I live," he said quietly. "It's too far. I won't have you driving back from there alone at this time of night."

"Where do you live?" she asked, loving the feel of his hand on hers.

He hesitated and for a moment she thought he was going to refuse to tell her. Did he expect that she was going to follow him home? "I've got a small ranch out in the Antelope Valley," he revealed at last. "It's about two hours from here."

"Well, there's only one thing to do, then," she said, taking a deep breath before she went on. "You'll have to spend the night at my place."

4

HE SAT STILL for a long time, playing with her fingers and avoiding her eyes. Finally he dropped her hand and sat back. "I don't know if that would be a very good idea, Marlo," he said evenly, his face a stony mask.

"Why not?" she asked, feeling that lump in her throat again. This was the first time she'd ever asked a man to spend the night—well, stay in her apartment, anyway—and it seemed as though he was going to turn her down.

He didn't answer for a moment, then shook his head, turning toward her. He leaned near, his face so close she could feel his breath on her cheek. "Are you trying to bribe me, lady?" he asked silkily.

Her eyes widened. "Wh-what?"

He was grinning, his roller-coaster change in moods throwing her off balance again. "I don't know what else to think. You've been trying to talk me into that modeling job for days, offering me cars and dinners and such." His eyes gleamed with devilment. "Now you're offering to make love to me."

Her jaw dropped and she didn't notice that the band had finished their set, leaving the room quiet. "Who said anything about making love?" she cried, much too loudly, then turned beet red as heads swiveled all around the room.

"Now you've done it," he chuckled. "You'll have every cowboy in the place in your office tomorrow morning, whether you want them or not."

She bit her lip. "Let's go," she whispered, avoiding eye contact with everyone in the restaurant.

"You're the boss," he said with subtle irony, pushing back his chair.

They left quickly, barely pausing to thank Martin and Rosie, and then they were out in the cool night air, walking toward her little car.

"Want me to drive?" he asked.

She considered it for a moment, but decided that would be giving him too much control. "No, I'll drive," she said, pulling out her keys and unlocking the passenger's door. "But you're going to have to tell me if we're going to the Antelope Valley, or to my apartment—" she pulled open the door with a snap of her wrist "—to sleep on my couch," she added emphatically.

"Sounds lonely," he said as he got into the car.

"But sensible," she retorted, plunking into the driver's seat.

He sighed. "No bribe?"

She gave him a glare for an answer.

The drive home was over quickly. Cal rattled off another amusing travelogue, keeping her in stitches all the way. It wasn't until she drove into her parking spot in the garage beneath the apartment building that his face changed.

"You do live alone, don't you?" His voice was still light, but she could sense a brooding quality beneath the humor. "I'm not going to have to fight off extraneous husbands or boyfriends or anything like that?"

She laughed, shaking her head. "Not even a room-mate," she reported. "Just you and me," she almost added, but it sounded so final put that way. She didn't want him to get ideas. Or did she?

They climbed the stairs to her level, and she could feel his mood changing, even though she couldn't really see his face. She'd been up stairs with men before. Not these stairs, but others like them. Usually they kept up a nervous patter as though hoping to keep her occupied so she wouldn't change her mind and send them off before they had their chance to make a play. Or else they tried to get cozy on the landing, setting the stage. But Cal seemed almost reluctant. What was he wary of?

She let him into her home, turning on the light as they entered. He came in behind her, not saying a word.

"This is it," she said, forcing a chattiness she didn't feel. "The couch is extra long, so I think it will fit even your tall frame. I'll get you some covers. If you want to take a shower or anything like that . . ."

Her voice trailed off. He wasn't listening. He stood at the large window that overlooked the courtyard and stared out into the night. The pool was lit up. It sparkled like a blue-green luminous jewel, but he didn't seem to see it. There was a turmoil in him; she could feel it.

Whirling on her toes, she stalked into the kitchen for a drink of water. What was with the man, anyway? One moment he was coaxing her into rollicking laughter, the next he looked like the spirit of Christmas past. She couldn't keep up with his mood swings, and she wasn't sure she wanted to try.

One quick night's sleep, she promised herself, *and then he's out of here.*

She plunked her glass down on the counter and turned to find him coming into the kitchen. He wanted to leave. She knew it. And she wanted very much to make him stay.

She moved quickly, reaching into a cupboard. "How about some coffee?" she said, feeling her heart beating in her throat.

There was a long, quivering silence, and then he let out a sigh that mixed oddly with a little laugh. "Decaffeinated?" he asked.

"You got it," she replied, relief washing through her in a bittersweet wave.

They took their mugs into the living room and sat down, he on the couch, she on a chair facing it. He stared silently into his coffee while she sat nervously on the edge of her seat, wondering where the warm feeling had flown.

It had been so nice, she realized on reflection. She'd never felt quite so special with a man before. That sense of pleasure had only come in flashes, to be banished again by his recurring preoccupation. But while it lasted, she'd felt close to him.

It had always been hard for her to get close to men. She'd had relationships off and on, some more intimate than others, but there'd always been something missing.

But there was something different with Cal. He smiled that cowboy smile, and it reached right through her barriers and touched a chord that seemed to let her senses flower. She wanted to open everything to him, to let him in where no man had ever been before. And then he shut down the warmth, and she was frightened again.

"What are you thinking about?" he asked suddenly, and she jumped, not about to tell him.

"I was thinking about how good you would look," she ad-libbed quickly, "in an advertisement featuring a cowboy hunkering down around a campfire, sipping hot coffee on a frosty night."

He stared at her for a moment, and then a smile began to creep into his eyes, seemingly despite his better judgment. "Only good?" he asked softly. "What happened to perfect?"

"Perfect is a goal," she said, "not a condition."

He laughed and his whole body seemed to relax. "I like you, Marlo," he said, as though the feeling were against his will. "You know what? You've never told me anything about what the Caron Man is supposed to be selling."

"You're right," she said. "I haven't."

He raised an eyebrow. "Is it a secret?"

She shook her head. "What do you think it might be?"

He paused. "Cigarettes? Beer? Whiskey?"

"You're not even close."

"Jeans? Men's cologne? A new brand of chili?"

She laughed. "No. The Caron corporation is an electronics firm."

"Electronics?" He frowned. "They want to use computers to round up cows?"

"Not exactly. The Caron Man will be wearing—and promoting—wrist radios."

He blinked at her. "What the heck are wrist radios? Are we talking Dick Tracy here?"

"Sort of." She jumped up from her chair. "I'll show you one." She rummaged in a desk drawer and came up with an object made of brightly colored plastic. "An AM-FM radio that you can strap to your wrist. Isn't it cute?"

"It is that." He held it and turned it in his hands. "But what does it have to do with cowboys?"

She laughed softly, sinking down on the couch beside him. "Nothing. Not yet. Not until I say it does."

"And you're not saying for now," he guessed accurately.

She nodded. "I want to get my entire presentation blocked out before I really say. My idea is sort of off-the-wall, and I don't want to blow it before I get things squared away."

He put the wrist radio down on the coffee table and turned toward her. "I like the way your eyes sparkle when you get into your work," he said, leaning back into the pillows. They were silent for a moment, watching each other. Marlo could feel something building between them, and it set her pulse on fire.

"I think I'd better go," he said abruptly, rising to his feet. "I can't stay here."

She rose beside him. "Why not?"

He ran a hand through his wiry hair. "You're a big girl, Marlo. You figure it out."

Marlo felt something new unfolding inside her. In the past she would have welcomed a man saying something like this. She would have smiled in gratitude, relieved to be rid of another explosive situation, relieved not to be put in a position of risk. The old Marlo would have quickly led Cal to the door. But this was a new Marlo. She didn't want him to go.

"Please stay," she said quietly, her gray eyes wide and vulnerable.

He groaned and reached out one finger to touch her cheek. "I can't promise you anything," he warned roughly.

She nodded. "I know."

He took her face in his hands and lowered his mouth to hers. She closed her eyes and let the moment sweep her away, let her own warmth, so soft, so moist, open to him, draw him in, curl around him like a seductive breeze.

His fingers slipped into her thick hair, gently kneading her scalp, and his lips moved against hers, tugging, stroking, caressing in a way that made the blood sing in her ears. His tongue explored, hers welcomed, and then the two of them became as one, each merged into a flowing dance of movement, of pleasing, of being pleased.

His kiss was heaven, all she could ever have imagined, and yet it wasn't enough. She could feel the urge for more in him, in herself. She wanted him tight against her, in her, all around. She wanted to consume him, to be consumed. She struggled for more of him as a drowning man struggling for air, and when his arms came around her, his hands searching for her softness, she tried to hide the pain they inflicted on her sunburn.

But even though she didn't make a sound, he could sense her discomfort. He drew away slowly, first his arms, then his chest, and finally, lingeringly, his lips. When she blinked up at him, her eyes misty with disappointment, he was chuckling.

"You might as well be wearing a chastity belt, honey," he told her. "There's no way I'm going to make love to you tonight."

"It doesn't hurt," she hastened to assure him, then flushed when she realized what she was doing. Begging—begging Cal to take her to bed. She could hardly believe it.

He turned her around, pushed down the straps of her cotton sundress and looked at the angry skin. "Have you put anything on this?" he asked.

"Just some lotion," she replied.

He made a cluck of disapproval. "That's no good. You need some good old-fashioned home remedy. Get naked."

"Get naked?" she repeated, eyeing him suspiciously. "Are you planning something kinky?"

"One girl's routine affair is another girl's kinkiness. I'll let you be the judge." He started for the kitchen.

"Where are you going?" She was so happy to have the warmth back that she wanted to follow him, to hold on to it.

"I think I can find what I need on my own. You go into your bedroom, take off your clothes and lie down on your tummy."

"Tummy?" she repeated to herself as she began to do as he'd ordered. But there was something comforting about the childish word. It gave her the confidence to go ahead and shed her dress and slip, even though a nervous tremble had begun to invade every part of her. Her strapless bra and underpants, however, stayed right where they were, and she pulled a sheet out of a drawer to wrap around her, then sat in the middle of the bed, legs crossed, terribly uneasy.

Cal scanned the room as he entered, taking in the delicate floral pattern on the spread and curtains, the collection of beautiful bottles on the dressing table, the

Seurat reproduction on the wall. Finally his attention focused on her, waiting on the bed trying to conceal her shudders. He came over and set down on her night-stand a washcloth and a bowl filled with a cloudy-looking concoction.

"What is it?" she asked apprehensively.

"I call it cowboy magic, myself. Will you go with that?"

She shook her head, holding the sheet against her. "I belong to the cynical generation," she told him. "We don't believe in magic. We like to see the ingredient list."

He picked the bowl up and swirled it under her nose. "I wish I could tell you it was made from ground bats' tongues and the sweat from angels' brows, but I've always been a truthful guy." He shook his head sadly. "It's baking soda and water. Satisfied?"

His gaze caught hers, and she felt a shiver of something scary, as the feeling she once got when the Ferris wheel broke down and she was all alone at the top. She pulled the sheet up under her chin as though that would protect her.

"So modest," he murmured, "for a woman who was so recently trying to seduce me."

"Trying to do what?" she asked indignantly, but he was already unwinding the sheet from around her, and she was letting him.

"What would you call it?" he asked, motioning her to lie down flat. He left the sheet around her from the waist down. "Throwing yourself at me. Asking me to spend the night."

She turned her head to watch him, hardly able to pay attention to what he was saying, she was so nervous about what he might be doing.

"Plying me with wrist radios," he went on, "and pretending that your sunburn didn't hurt."

"Ouch," she said when the washcloth first touched her skin, but it was more a reaction of anxiety than real pain. He dipped the cloth into the solution and wiped it ever so gently against her, stroking first her neck, then down toward her shoulder blades, her arms. Gradually she relaxed, letting the liquid soothe her. It felt cool and there was no sting at all.

"Ordinarily, I'm not such a seducible guy," Cal continued, his voice a purring background noise. "I've turned down women who could melt the Ice Age." His fingers sneaked beneath the band of her bra, and suddenly she felt it release. She stiffened, but then relaxed again as he continued his refreshing cure across her back. "But there's something in those big, soft eyes of yours, Miss Marlo Santee," he went on smoothly, beginning to pull away the sheet that still wrapped her hips, "that seems to put a stranglehold on my libido."

Her high-cut swimsuit had exposed the tender skin at the top of her thighs. She felt his fingers slipping beneath the silky material of her panties to make way for the washcloth. She held her breath, closing her eyes fiercely, holding back the tingling sensation his touch engendered. Suddenly, without any warning, she began to giggle.

"You find that amusing?" he asked ruefully.

"No." She giggled again, then burst into laughter. "But this situation is. Don't you think we're a silly-looking pair? You fully dressed and me lying here almost naked—and we hardly know each other!"

His voice held a threat of irony. "Sometimes that's the best way," he replied. "Flip over."

"What?" She went very still. Her naked back was all very well, but did she dare expose her front to him quite this shamelessly? "I'm not as badly burned on the front...."

"Flip over."

She clutched the loose bra to her breasts as she complied, and it was his turn to be amused. "Pretend we know each other better if that will make you feel more comfortable," he suggested, beginning to dab the solution across her collarbone. "Pretend we've known each other for years."

She glanced at him, then avoided his eyes, looking around the room at anything, everything else. "We could try Instant Intimacy," she said.

"Sounds like a new soup."

"It's an antidote for the rootless Californian," she said, squirming as his moving cloth tickled her. "What you do is tell a whole string of facts about yourself, things you like, very quickly. Then the other reciprocates."

"Okay," he agreed, moving down to her legs. "Give me an example."

"All right." She closed her eyes, trying to concentrate and forget where he was touching. "Gershwin and *The King and I*." This wasn't as easy as it had sounded when Peter had done it. Maybe he'd had a lot of practice. She thought hard. "Hot fudge sundaes. Pizza after a football game." It started coming easier. "A roaring fire on a cold afternoon. Snowflakes on Christmas Eve." Too easily. It was pulling up painful images from the past. "Climbing roses. A child waiting on the steps for her father to come home from work." Her voice was beginning to shake. "Red tile roofs. A father and son playing ball in the park. Kittens. Newborn babies."

Two fat, hot tears were squeezing out between her black lashes. Where on earth had they come from? She tried to blink them away, but she was pretty sure Cal had seen them. A sudden picture of her father's face flashed before her, and she hardened her heart, forcing back the sorrow.

"Thunderheads over the desert." Cal had picked up the thread without her having to urge him. "Tumbleweed piled up against a fence. A wild mustang high on a mesa. Rain on your face. Cottonwoods in a summer breeze. Mesquite burning." He paused, and when he said the last item, there was a smile in his voice. "Red tile roofs."

She met his gaze and smiled back. She wondered if he realized how lonely his list sounded. It was obvious he loved the wilderness, loved the great outdoors, and didn't need anyone else to enhance his enjoyment. A melancholy shiver went through her, a feeling of hopelessness.

And then she let her mind wander to her own list. What had that shown? She thought back over it and almost sat up in surprise. Home and family, that was what it sounded like. Marlo Santee, career woman? Was she losing her mind? Those were all things she'd turned her back on long ago. She knew how much it hurt to lose them. She would never let herself be that vulnerable again.

"Cal?" she asked, not really sure why, but suddenly aware that the movement of his cloth had stopped, that he was leaning back, looking at her body with hooded eyes.

He didn't answer. His fingers were hard and firm as he took away the bra, tossing it aside. She started to sit up, but his hand had already cupped one breast, sending a wave of shock and excitement through her core.

"Cal!" she said with a gasp, but she wasn't forcing him away. Her hands went into his hair, clutching, pulling him more tightly against her. There was a new sort of trembling in her legs, a new sort of hunger in her soul, a new sort of desire in her body.

I want him, she realized. *I want him now.*

Somehow she knew that he could show her love as she'd never known it, that he could give her a sense of her womanhood such as she'd never dreamed. And now that she'd glimpsed that possibility, she didn't want to lose it.

His mouth came to her lips, hot and moist and throbbing with need for fulfillment. She answered with her own demand, reaching for him, wanting to show him how much she wanted him to stay. But it wasn't enough.

He groaned and pulled away, rising to his feet in a jerky motion. "I've got to get out of here," he said roughly. "I'll go get some fresh air."

"Where are you going?" she asked, getting up and pulling the sheet to her chest. Her black hair swirled around her in an ebony cloud, and her lips were red with the evidence of his kiss.

"I don't know," he replied without looking back. "Maybe I'll drown myself in your pool." Then he was gone, and in a moment she heard the apartment door slam.

She sat very still for a long, long moment, then jumped up, reaching for her clothes. She stopped with her bra half fastened. What did she think she was doing? Was she going to run after him?

Slowly she pulled it off again and searched instead for her nightgown. Maybe he wasn't coming back. Maybe he had a friend nearby. Maybe he'd take a taxi home. Whatever he did, she couldn't sit around and moon over him. She had to go to bed and get some sleep. Tomorrow was another day of work, and it didn't promise to be a pleasant one.

Leaving the door unlocked just in case, she went to bed. But not to sleep. She lay for almost an hour, staring at the darkness in the room, trying to understand what was happening to her.

She'd always been so cautious, so sensible. She'd had relationships, but only on her own terms. Always with someone whose work and outlook were similar to hers. Someone cool and calm. She wasn't hot-blooded, and she'd never wanted a hot-blooded man.

She closed her eyes and remembered how she'd turned to fire at Cal's touch. There was a passion in him that she couldn't resist, a passion that became her own when she was with him. How could that be? She'd never fallen this way before.

Not in love, of course, she hastened to reassure herself. She wouldn't do anything that stupid. But she had fallen into something. Something she didn't know how to handle. She hugged her arms around herself tightly and tried to go to sleep.

And then he was back. She heard him come in the front door, and she held her breath, waiting. She'd left a light on in the living room, and when he came to the door of her bedroom, he filled it like a huge shadow.

"If you still want me to, I'll be your Caron Man," he said.

She groped for words. "That—that's wonderful."

"You don't have to use my name, do you?"

"N-no. I don't know why your name would matter." She could hardly believe it. What had changed his mind?

"Okay. When do I start?"

She swallowed, wishing she knew how to thank him. "Tomorrow."

"Fine."

He left the doorway, and in a few moments the light went out in the living room. It was dark. Time to sleep. But the sky was turning purple in the east before Marlo closed her eyes.

5

IT SEEMED she had barely fallen asleep when a movement forced her awake again. But not fully awake, just enough to sense a presence in her room.

She turned over, sighing deeply. She didn't want to open her eyes. She was so, so tired. She just wanted to be left alone, to sleep.

He slipped beneath her blankets as silently as the moon shadows spread across her windowsill. She smiled, not opening her eyes, not turning to greet him. She wanted to sleep, but she wanted him, too. Greedy, she thought with hazy inattention. Greedy for everything she'd never had.

She felt his smooth hands gather her thick hair and lift it, and then his lips were caressing the tender skin of her neck, searching out the most sensitive spots with his tingling kisses. She stretched happily, arching to his touch. His breath was hot and arousing on her neck, stirring the tiny hairs, sending sensations of delight down her back. She was warm, sizzling, bursting with a new sense of her own needs, and the sheets were cool and crisp against her.

His hand cupped her breast, then began to slide across the silky nothing of her nightgown, following the contours of her body, exploring, enjoying, awakening her senses. He bent over her, his breath fresh and minty, his heartbeat loud and urgent. She still hadn't opened her eyes. She was waiting, anticipating, drifting with the wind.

His hard fingers touched her knee, and then she could feel him beginning to bunch up the folds of her night-gown, tugging at the hem, slipping it higher, higher, releasing her from its confines and into his possession. She turned toward him willingly, moaning a soft en-dearment . . .

"Marlo!"

She stopped very still, holding her breath, her eyes squeezed shut.

"Marlo. It's getting late."

Slowly, reluctantly, she opened her eyes. Cal was standing in the doorway, his shirt still unbuttoned, his hair still tousled from his night's sleep.

"I'll bet even account executives are expected to get into the office before noon," he said dryly. "Aren't they?"

She scrunched down as far as she could into the cov-ers, so that only her huge gray eyes and her sweep of jet-black hair was visible. Her cheeks were burning. What a dream! Could he tell? Had he heard her? Had she called out his name? She stared at him, afraid to wonder what he was thinking, and he stared back per-ceptively.

He knew. She was sure of it. Embarrassment coursed through her.

Suddenly he grinned and the tension dissolved. "Come on, sleepyhead," he said. "I've got breakfast ready."

"What?" She propped herself up on one elbow. "Where did you learn to cook?"

He threw her a look of mock indignation. "What do you think I am, a mindless gorilla? Anyone living on his own for as long as I have who didn't learn to fend for himself would starve to death." He smiled in a way that said they were friends, if not lovers. "Come on. I'll have a cup of coffee waiting for you. I don't want to be late on my first day at work." And he turned away from her doorway, heading for the kitchen.

At least she hadn't dreamed that, she told herself as she showered, then scrambled into a simple beige linen suit.

"Will you be able to juggle this with your ranch work?" she asked as she came out into the kitchen.

"No problem," he told her, ushering her into the place of honor he'd set for her at the table. "I've got a friend handling things while I'm gone."

After a hurried and surprisingly delicious breakfast of scrambled eggs, bacon and toast, she dropped Cal off at the garage where his car was being fixed and went on to work by herself. She wouldn't need him until the afternoon, so she made plans to meet him after lunch.

She entered the outer office to find Jeri waiting for her. Her assistant had obviously taken her advice and had spent the previous evening outfitting herself for action on the rodeo front. Her shirt was bright orange and embroidered in golden jute trim, her skirt forest green and fringed. She wore shiny new cowboy boots as well. But her expression didn't match her zany outfit. She was definitely displeased.

"Look at what's going on in there!" she cried, pointing an accusing finger toward the inner office.

Marlo frowned and hurried in. There was Ted Hanford, straightening the picture on her wall.

"Ted, what do you think you're doing?" Marlo demanded, hands on her hips.

"Be Prepared is more than just a motto with me," he told her cheerfully, stepping back and squinting at the painting. "You know, I like your ocean scene, but I think my own fox hunt oil will look a lot snazzier." He looked at the far wall. "I'll put my trophy case right over there, don't you think? Where the clients can see all my badges of victory. Gives them confidence." He sighed happily. "I'm going to like it here, I think."

Marlo knew he was trying to shake her confidence. But she knew Ted and his tricks. He'd had no word from Mr. Grayson, or he would be doing a lot more than speculating.

Jeri came up next to Marlo, her face as stern as an angry bulldog. "Just give me the word," she threatened, one hand clenched in a fist, "just give me the word, and I'll paste him one."

Watching the two of them, Marlo almost laughed aloud. Ted's attempts at psychological warfare struck her as amusing today. She was on top of the world.

The situation seemed to entertain Ted as well. "Why, Jeri," he said in a tone guaranteed to raise her hackles. "What's with the threats? Is this to go with your new Annie Oakley image?" He gestured toward her bright Western wear.

Jeri's lower jaw came out even farther. "Annie Oakley always got her man," she ground out. "Right between the eyes if necessary." She jerked with her thumb. "Scram, buster."

Ted looked her up and down with his penetrating stare. Something mysterious flickered there for a moment, but it was quickly gone again. He turned to leave, but paused as he came abreast of Marlo. "Just don't let her wear a sunbonnet," he advised, sotto voce and ogling Jeri significantly. "She'd be so darned cute I'd have to break down and ask her for a date." Smiling in triumph as Jeri panted her outrage, he left.

"He's always making fun of me," Jeri cried, ready to run after him with claws unsheathed.

"No, no, no." Marlo stopped her, then couldn't help but laugh. "He's just doing whatever he can to get your goat. Don't you see that? And when you get angry, he wins." Jeri still sputtered and Marlo shook her head. "Believe me, darling, he's succeeding marvelously. If you want to get back at him, don't react!"

"How can I not react to that infuriating stuffed shirt?"

Marlo shrugged, letting go now that she was fairly sure Jeri wouldn't chase Ted down the hall. "Just learn to take it easy," she advised cheerfully. She went to her desk and began straightening things, humming as she worked.

Jeri stood and stared at her. "You're humming," she accused.

Marlo looked up. "Am I?" She smiled. "So I am."

"You're happy," Jeri said, as though that were something one shouldn't mention in public.

Marlo considered, holding a pencil to her cheek. "Not happy exactly," she mused.

Jeri snorted. "It looks like happy to me. What's up?"

Marlo grinned, savoring the suspense. "I just hope those cowboy clothes are returnable," she said. "You're not going to Phoenix."

"What is it?" Jeri insisted. "Tell me!"

"It's a surprise. Make an appointment with Angel Cortez in the art department for after lunch. I'll show you there." She was enjoying Jeri's consternation. "We're going to begin work right away."

Jeri gasped. "You found someone?"

Marlo raised her chin and said teasingly, "You'll see."

THE MORNING SEEMED to fly by, and she was too excited to eat, so she worked right through the lunch hour. She passed Ted in the hall and gave him such a wide grin he stopped and watched her walk by. Marlo chuckled. It felt good to be within reach of success again.

She met Jeri outside the art department.

"Well, here I am," Jeri announced.

"And not a moment too soon," Marlo responded sunnily, though nervousness was beginning to fray the edges of her good humor.

"So what's the big surprise?"

"You'll see." Marlo paused at the glass door. Now that she'd arrived, she found herself hesitating to take the final plunge. What if Cal hadn't shown up? What if he'd changed his mind? What if he came and hated it?

There was such a wariness in him. She knew that he didn't want to get involved with her. She also knew that involvement was going to be inevitable if he worked for her. Six months together without something happening? Impossible? That certainly was both a promise and a curse. She feared it almost as much as she anticipated it. But somehow a strong feeling of destiny rode with this step. If he were here waiting in Angel's office, she knew her fate.

"Well, I'm looking as hard as I can, but I still can't see," Jeri twitted her gently.

"Okay." She took a deep breath. "Here we go." She opened the art department door, and the two of them strode toward Angel Cortez's studio.

Angel opened his door right away to their knock, and there was Cal in the middle of the room, looking like a younger version of John Wayne.

"You came!" she breathed, seeing only him. She felt like a teenager greeting her date for the prom.

He raised a dark brow. "You didn't believe me?"

She shrugged happily, hardly noticing Jeri's delighted whoops. Even in the glaring light of the room, he looked wonderful. He carried his slightly scruffy riding clothes and Stetson with such an air of dignified authenticity she could almost feel the prairie in his blood. "You're just so perfect," she said softly.

"How did you do it?" Jeri was yelling. "I can't believe it!" She turned excitedly, and Angel Cortez moved away as though he were afraid she was about to hug him in celebration.

Angel was a bearlike man who seemed larger than he was. From his appearance no one would dream he did the most intricate, meticulous oil paintings Marlo had ever seen. He wore a bland expression that belied the sharp intelligence lurking beneath the exterior. This was the first time Marlo had worked with him, but she knew he had a good reputation, and she was hoping for the best.

Right now Angel was looking from Marlo to Cal with a frown, noting the way their eyes locked. It was obvious there was more between them than a professional relationship. He almost said something about it, then stopped and turned back to his work, politely shoving the excitable Jeri from the scene. "Get out of here," he told her gruffly. "We're working."

Jeri went, but not before she gave Marlo an exaggerated A-OK sign.

Angel had Cal sitting on a crude mock-up of a horse. Marlo circled it slowly. "Isn't he perfect?" she repeated to Angel as she neared where he was sketching.

"He's all right," he said grudgingly, glancing at her as though he weren't too sure of her sanity. "You want to take a look at some of these ideas?"

They went over different layouts Angel had worked out, some with Cal on a horse, some with him at a campfire, one with him carrying a saddle over his shoulders. Marlo was suddenly all business, and when she looked at Cal, it was with the eye of a practiced professional.

"How about style and tone?" Angel asked once she'd pinpointed a few poses she wanted recreated on film. "As I see it, you're going from dreams and memories, a hearkening back to a bygone age. I visualize muted images, soft colors, soft edges."

Marlo shook her head decisively. "I've given that a lot of thought, and I get your point, but I disagree." She narrowed her eyes and watched Cal objectively. "I didn't search this hard to find the right man only to lose him in shadows." She waved a hand at him, willing Angel to understand. "He's real. He's strong and he's hard and he's dependable. That's what I want to get across. Just the cowboy image he represents will be enough to bring on the dreams. I want pictures that are bright and hard edged and clear as a bell to convey the rest." She waved her hand again. "Clear and simple truth. No tricks. No gimmicks."

Angel shrugged. "You're the boss."

The door opened and a female employee peered around it. She looked quickly around the room, saw Cal, then disappeared. It turned out to be only one of many such visits. The word was out, and most of the typing pool came to check out the "hunk" in the art department. Even Mary Jane, a secretary who lived in Marlo's apartment building, dropped by. She gave Marlo a casual wave, then hung around for ten minutes, absolutely unashamed of her interest.

Marlo began to wonder whether she dared leave Cal alone, but there was work to be done. She went off to do some paperwork in an adjoining room, and when she came back, she had two of Angel's assistants in tow and a list of decisions to be made.

"We're trying to pick a location," she told Cal. "Do you have any suggestions?"

"That depends," he said slowly. "Are you looking for flatland or mountains?"

She thought for a moment. She knew cowboys herded cattle on flatland, but mountains looked so rugged. Besides, she didn't want any pictures of cows. "Mountains," she decided.

He nodded. "Then I'd say we ought to look for a place that gives the feel of the Sierras."

She nodded. "You're right." She turned to one of Angel's assistants. "Can you get together a list of mountain locations by next week?" Her eyes brightened as the idea took hold. "We can't go all out on the comprehensives, but for the final shoot we should search for some place like Yosemite where we can helicopter in."

Cal changed his position, ignoring Angel's scowl. He flexed his wide shoulders and grimaced. "You going to need me again before the actual pictures are taken?"

Marlo opened her mouth to answer, but Angel beat her to the punch, his eyes gleaming with mischief. "Sure will," he said with relish. "We'll need you every day this week."

Marlo could see the mood that was building in Cal, and she hurried to forestall it. "Only in the afternoons, I think. We'll try to schedule all the consultations for afternoons." She smiled at him brightly. "And it would be helpful if you could come to the presentation next week."

"Consultations?" Cal frowned. "What consultations?"

Angel laughed for the first time that afternoon. "Oh, you'll really like those," he said heartily. "You'll be in on all the big decisions, like what fabric looks best against your skin and what color brings out the highlights in your hair. And, of course, Marlo will need you with her for the conference with the photographer, so they can get the lighting right, etcetera." He paused for effect. "And, best of all, there'll be the conference with the hairstylist and the makeup artist." He nodded wisely. "Listen, they can be a model's best friends. You're going to need to establish a real rapport there. Makeup is important."

"Makeup?" Cal said the word as though it were a disease he didn't want to catch. "You didn't say anything about makeup." His eyes hardened, and Marlo could see disaster on the horizon.

"Don't worry," she said quickly, wishing she had the nerve to kick Angel. "I'm sure we won't need to use much makeup on you."

"Yeah," Angel said dryly. "He's already so perfect."

His last word hung in the air, which was suddenly very still. Cal turned slowly toward him, and though there was nothing concrete Marlo could put her finger on, she could feel the new sense of danger in him. She found herself holding her breath while the two men stared at each other.

"You got what you want yet?" Cal asked, his voice soft and emotionless.

"Uh, no," Angel mumbled, looking down at his sketch pad. "I'm going to need quite a few more poses actually."

He went back to work, and Cal relaxed a bit. Marlo took a deep breath and was thankful it hadn't gone any further. It was all her fault, she realized belatedly. She'd been such a fool, expecting everyone else to join in her joy over Cal. Of course that would put other people's backs up. How could she have expected anything else? She'd have to be more careful in the future.

At the same time she could see that Cal was getting more and more restless. She knew he wasn't going to last much longer. "Can't we let him go?" she whispered to Angel.

"Not yet."

She knew he was right. If they let Cal go now, they'd just have to call him back later. It might be better to get as much accomplished as possible before his mood worsened. She wished she could think of something to help the time pass more pleasantly for him.

Suddenly her eye fell on a guitar propped against the wall in the corner. "A guitar!" she breathed.

Angel followed her line of vision and nodded. "That's mine. I play it sometimes to relax."

"May we borrow it?" She strode forward, not waiting for an answer. "Let's see how he looks playing it."

He looked just great. In fact, he strummed the strings as though they were old friends.

"Get a couple of poses of this," Marlo demanded excitedly.

Angel grunted, doing as he was told, but his expression wasn't sunny.

"Play something," she said. "Can you sing, too?"

"Sure." With a playful twang in his voice, he obliged.

Don't treat me like a lover, baby,
Treat me like a friend,
Cuz love with you is terminal,
And friendship never ends.

Marlo made a face. "How about something more—"

"Romantic?" Cal looked at her steadily, and she probably should have noticed the devilish light in his eyes.

"Yes," she said, flushing slightly. "Romantic."

"Anything you say, ma'am," he drawled, pushing his hat back on his head. His mustache hid his grin, but the corners of his eyes crinkled.

He played a few chords, and Marlo leaned back, arms folded, enjoying the lovely melody. When he began to sing, his voice was low and husky, just as she'd

known it would be. The tune was country and western, and she swayed a bit to the beat.

She walks by, so softly, and says
Hey boy, you're doin' fine,

He sang with country softness, his eyes holding hers.

And she don't know my heart twists,
Cuz she's got me on her line.
I'm just a guy who works here,
And she's my lady boss.

The fact that his eyes were twinkling wickedly had
finally sunk in. Alarmed, Marlo straightened, wondering how to stop the song before things got worse.
But she was too late. Cal was really into it now, and
nothing was going to stem the flow. His blue gaze chal-
lenged her to try.

But someday I'll show her,
No matter what the cost,
That I'm—

His grin stretched dramatically, and his voice rose to
fill the room, not quite drowning out the chuckles of the
rest of his audience.

—crazy for her laughter,
I burn to taste her smile,
I know by lookin' at her,
That her love will be so—

"Cal!" Marlo grabbed the guitar from him in mid-note, her cheeks flaming. "You made the whole thing up!"

He gave her a phony look of injured dignity. "That's one of your typical cowboy talents, boss lady. Making up songs to lull the cattle."

"Scratch the guitar," she muttered, marching across the room to put it back in the corner and trying to ignore the snickers from the others. "We'll stick to the horse."

This wouldn't do. People mustn't get the idea she was involved with Cal. That could ruin everything. She was out to improve her image here at Grayson's. Consorting with a model would do nothing to help.

She walked over and scrutinized the pictures Angel had sketched while Cal held the guitar.

"How do you like these?" Angel asked. "I think they're the best yet."

She agreed immediately. "Hey," she said. "These are great." She took one over to show Cal.

He nodded. "It does occur to me, however," he said calmly, "that a cowboy playing the guitar won't be listening to a wrist radio."

"Oh," she said, crushed. "You're right."

Suddenly they were all laughing, even Marlo, and the tension that had filled the room from the beginning evaporated.

Things were better after that, but Cal looked more and more strained as time went by. At one point Angel took a phone call, and Marlo moved closer to Cal. "How are you doing?"

He moved restlessly and finally stood, flexing his legs. "I feel like a damned giraffe on a merry-go-round," he said grumpily. He shook his head. "I've got to admit this isn't exactly my idea of a fun afternoon." He saw her look of distress and relaxed. "But I'll live through it," he assured her.

"You'd rather be out riding the range, like a real cowboy, wouldn't you?"

He gazed at her speculatively, then grazed her cheek with his forefinger, touching her ever so softly. "How about you, lovely lady?" he asked, his voice a low rumble. "Would you like to go out and ride the range with me?"

Marlo laughed, but she was slightly shocked by the suggestion. It seemed so absurd. "Me? I've never been on a horse."

"I'll take you sometime," he said, his eyes smoky with some unnamed emotion. "I'll show you what it's like and teach you all you need to know."

Teach her all she needed to know. She was sure he could, and not only on a horse. She blinked rapidly, trying to keep her mind on the conversation and not on the currents running beneath. "I—I'm not so sure I'm going to like it," she warned him.

Amusement bubbled in his voice, as though he knew her dilemma. "I'll make you like it."

"You will?"

"I will." He paused, but she couldn't look away. She was trapped, and though he wasn't holding her, she couldn't have broken free if she tried.

"I'll turn you into a cowgirl," he said gently. "You just wait and see." His smile was sardonic. "You've got to come. You owe me, after all this. If it weren't for you, I wouldn't be doing this, you know."

She knew that was true. He was no model, and he wasn't taking to the work. She tried to smile jauntily. "I was a good persuader, wasn't I?"

"That's not what I mean." His eyes darkened and he moved a little closer. "I'm doing this for you and for you only." His huge hand cupped her chin, tilting her face up toward his. "You know that."

She was captivated, speechless. She'd been sure it would happen eventually, but it had begun already. His wariness was evaporating, and her willingness was growing. As she stared up into his eyes, she saw his determination. He wanted her. That certainly sent a thrill through her system.

The telephone rang again, and Angel picked it up. This time the call was for her.

"All hands on deck," Jeri cried into her ear. "The storm isn't over yet."

"What's up?"

"Phillipa just called. Mr. Grayson wants to see you right away. He's got two copywriters in his office, and I don't have to name them for you, do I?"

"Oh, boy." Marlo sighed. "I'll get up there right away. You hold the fort until I get back."

"Don't you mean take the helm?" Jeri quipped. "We can't go mixing our metaphors."

"Whatever. Just be there in case I need you."

"To help pack?"

"To help hold this project together!"

She put down the receiver and frowned, thinking fast. It seemed Jill and Ted had stepped up their little war. She wished she knew just what their plan of attack was today, so she could prepare a counterattack.

If Mr. Grayson were directly involved, it sounded serious. She bit her lip.

Cal watched her. "This is something serious, isn't it?" he said at last.

Her eyes widened. She'd almost forgotten he was there, and he noted that fact. "Oh, yes," she replied. "I may be fighting for my life here."

"Are you going to win?" he asked quietly.

"You'd better believe it!" She turned away, not noticing the frown that clouded his face as he watched her go. Her mind was completely absorbed by the fight to come. She didn't have room for anything else.

6

ART GRAYSON'S OFFICE was as gloomily lit as ever, but Marlo hardly noticed. She was busy steeling herself to confront the two copywriters who sat before the desk.

"Sit down, Marlo," Mr. Grayson said. "We've got trouble."

Clutching her folder, she sank to the edge of a chair, poised and ready for the attack that would come. Jill Nettles was slim and intense, watching everything with bright, birdlike eyes. Ted was above it all as usual. He sat back knowingly, as though the world was a tremendous joke and he was the only one in on the punch line.

"These two are complaining," Art told her bluntly. "They say you're scuttling the Caron account." He put up a hand to keep her from breaking in. "I've been hearing rumors for a couple of weeks, but I was hoping you'd come through for us, Marlo. Now Jill and Ted tell me that's not happening." He frowned. It was obvious he didn't like having to deal with failure. "They tell me Mr. Caron is being put off daily. That you've postponed the presentation twice. That you're floundering for ideas, but reject everything they offer. That you won't even fill them in on your progress."

So much of it was true, so many of the details correct, that Marlo was stymied for a moment. But she wasn't floundering at all. In fact, she'd never been surer of a concept. But how could she convey that to her boss? She didn't have enough concrete evidence to make a strong case for herself.

"We did have a few problems," she admitted. "I couldn't find the right model, and then when I did find him, I couldn't convince him to do the ad—"

"Inexperience will always show through," Jill sniffed.

"But everything's been resolved," Marlo added hurriedly. "We've scheduled a presentation for a week from Friday."

Art didn't look convinced. "This is an important account, Marlo. I trusted you."

Her heart sank. She couldn't stand to disappoint him like this. How could she explain that she had a great ad campaign in the offing? She paused a little too long before answering, and he pulled some papers off his desk. "Here are some of the suggestions Ted made, suggestions you turned down." He gazed at them and shrugged. "They look fine to me."

Marlo took a deep breath. The only real revenge was success. "Caron came to us because they wanted a new direction, a new position in the marketplace. Ted's copy was targeted to the same old children's market. I wanted something completely different. And so did Mr. Caron." She waved a hand toward the papers Art held. "That's the same stuff Caron was getting at their old ad agency. If they'd wanted that, they'd have stayed there. But that old approach doesn't work."

Jill blinked her eyes rapidly. "What do you mean it doesn't work? It works for similar products. Just ask Research!"

Marlo turned to her earnestly, trying to explain. "That's just it. It worked all right, but it didn't give Caron the market share they wanted. Mr. Caron wants to break out of the pack, and to do that we have to go a new way. Don't you see? They needed new positioning, a new brand image."

"Cowboys?" Ted asked. "That's the new brand image for an electronics firm?" He smiled scornfully.

Everyone stared at Marlo. "Cowboys?" Mr. Grayson asked at last, his voice toneless. "You're giving them cowboys?"

"Children don't even like cowboys anymore," Jill put in. "They like robots and soldiers and space. There aren't any cowboy movies or Western series on television. Kids don't even know what cowboys and Indians are. My nine-year-old nephew thinks wampum is something you do to the other guy in a good fight. The old West is dead. Just ask Research."

Marlo could feel the hostility building. She shook her head, trying to fend it off. "But don't you see," she said, wishing her voice wouldn't shake, "that's irrelevant. We're not targeting children. We're not going for the kiddie magazines and the afternoon cartoons. That's been done. This time we're aiming higher. We're hitting the grandmother market."

There was stunned silence around the room, although her aim surely shouldn't have been news to Jill and Ted. She'd tried to hammer it home often enough. They just hadn't listened.

Finally Mr. Grayson frowned. "Do you mean—"

"I mean there are a lot of grandmothers who have more discretionary cash than young parents do." Marlo sat forward on her chair. "These grandmothers will quickly see the value of our wrist radios for their grandchildren, once they are aware of them. The problem is to make them aware in an attractive way."

She paused and no one tried to interrupt. That was a good sign. She wished, fleetingly, that she'd brought Cal along. One look at him would have convinced them. Instead, she began passing out the sketches Angel had made. "There are plenty of people," she went on, "who still have a romantic image of the West. This ad is meant to appeal to them. But it's also targeting the generation that grew up with Dick Tracy, people who think that wrist radios are a pretty neat concept." She flashed a smile. "The target has always been the children themselves before. Well, those children are inundated with space toys and far-out gadgets. The wrist radio probably seems fairly tame to them. They see better things on their average afternoon cartoon. But the older generation still has a warm spot for wrist radios. They're the ones we want to sell those to."

The silence that greeted her was a victory of sorts. Still, Jill had a volley or two left in her canon. "But that still doesn't excuse her of ignoring our copy," she claimed weakly.

Marlo wouldn't concede anything. "I had to ignore your copy because you ignored the direction I wanted that copy to go."

"You're an account executive now, Marlo, not a copywriter," Mr. Grayson reminded her. "You've got to learn to let go of things, let someone else do it."

"I've tried to, but—"

"You didn't!" Jill almost shrieked.

Mr. Grayson stopped the bickering with a toss of his head. "You've got the research to back you up?" he demanded.

That was a sore spot. If Marlo admitted she was going solely on her own intuition, she'd be dead. "Research hasn't come through yet," she admitted reluctantly. "They've done the legwork, but just haven't got the statistics compiled yet."

Art stood, effectively dismissing them all. "I want the numbers, and I want them tomorrow," he ordered.

Jill rose, her eyes wide with outrage. Ted put a hand on her elbow and began to guide her out the door. "Save your energy for the next battle," he said with his ever-present sardonic humor. "We've lost this one."

It seemed he was right about the battle. Heaven only knew how the war would turn out. Marlo hurried back to her office and got Jeri on the phone to the research department right away. She needed numbers and she needed them fast. When they continued to drag their feet, she raced up to the tenth floor to put a fire under them herself.

It was late when she finally headed back to her office. The elevator was crowded, and when it stopped at the next floor, more people shoved their way on board. Two of them happened to be Ted and Jill, and Marlo held her breath as they squeezed in, one on either side of her.

"It would appear that tight squeezes are your specialty," Ted said under his breath.

"Just like putting the squeeze on is yours," she snapped back.

He chuckled appreciatively, but before he could go on, the elevator stopped at yet another floor, and Marlo found herself staring into Cal's bright-blue eyes.

He looked more Western than ever, a startling contrast to the steel-and-glass structure where everyone dressed in gabardine and linen. He looked rough. Beautifully rough. Untouched and untamed. Her heart leaped into her throat at the sight of him.

There was no question of his coming aboard; there was simply no more room. But that didn't seem to be on his agenda anyway. "Hey, lady," he said softly, "going my way?"

She didn't even notice the wariness in his eyes again—that this question was, perhaps, more important than the casual observer might suspect. All she saw was the man she was beginning to count on, the man who made her feel like a woman. She needed him, needed the escape he represented, the relief from pressure.

She stared up at him, and suddenly all the bustle and tension didn't matter anymore. Nothing mattered except being with him.

"Anything you say, cowboy," she replied, stepping off the elevator and into his arms. And he leaned down and kissed her briefly on the lips.

The elevator stayed there for another moment, as though it were as shocked as the people inside. There wasn't a sound from the crowd, but she could feel the disbelief. The doors purred shut, and she almost expected someone to open them again, so they could all finish watching the scene.

Cal curled an arm around her shoulders, and they began to walk toward the stairway. She felt a warm bubble of happiness at being with him. But she couldn't help thinking about what had just happened. Her two adversaries were probably going to burn up the hall-ways in their haste to get to Grayson's office with tales of how she was using the cowboy theme because she was romancing a cowboy. But for now she didn't care. She didn't care about anything but the warm, protec-tive arms around her and the hard, weather-beaten face smiling down at her.

"Where are we going?" she asked once they'd found Cal's newly repaired Mustang in the parking lot.

"To dinner."

She watched his strong tanned hands on the wheel as they smoothly turned a corner. He hadn't asked if she were busy. He hadn't even allowed for the possibility.

"You just take over, don't you?" she said, a tiny smile turning up the corners of her mouth. "I thought I was the one who hired you."

"Just fitting my Western image, ma'am," he said in the thick drawl he'd used when she'd first met him. A red light caught them, and he turned toward her, pull-ing her close for a quick but effective kiss. "You want macho? I can give you macho."

There'd never been a doubt in her mind. The taste of his rough kiss stung her lips and she wanted more.

"I don't want macho at all," she protested. But deep inside she had to admit macho had its appeal, as long as it didn't go too far. She liked the way he kissed her. She liked the way he'd taken her off the elevator. She even liked the way he was taking over her evening. *Let's face it, Marlo*, she said to herself, still watching him, *you like him a lot. More, probably, than anyone else you've ever been with.*

They turned onto Venice Boulevard, and she knew they were heading for the beach, but she didn't ask for specifics. Every mile they traveled seemed to put more distance between them and the problems she'd left behind at work. She could feel her body relaxing, her mind lightening. Looking at Cal, she wished the car had a bench seat instead of the buckets they were sitting in. She wanted to be nearer. She was tempted to reach out and touch him, to run a hand through his hair as he drove. But she didn't quite have the nerve.

"You, too?" he growled and she jumped.

"Me, too, what?" she asked.

He slid a long glance her way, then returned his attention to his driving. "Staring at me. I've had people staring at me all day. I'm about stared out."

"Oh, I'm sorry." She bit her lip, holding back a chuckle. "I didn't know that being stared at was such hard work."

"It is," he stated firmly. "I've been fresher after a day of laying fence than I am right now."

"That's what you get for being so perfect," she told him.

He growled and Marlo laughed. "I won't stare at you anymore, I promise." She put her hands over her eyes. "But it's going to be tough. And you're going to feel a bit silly leading me around by the elbow."

She felt the car stop and the engine die, and she peeked through her fingers. "Caught you!" Cal announced. "What kind of a woman can't even keep a promise for more than thirty seconds?"

But he was smiling, and she dropped her hands. "I just can't help it," she said softly. "You're irresistible."

He held her gaze for a long moment, his smile slowly fading. Then he looked away restlessly. "We're here," he said as he got out of the car.

Marlo surveyed their surroundings. They'd parked beside a beachside restaurant with a spectacular view of the ocean. "I'm famished," she said as she reached for her door handle.

"Good." He pulled open her door and helped her out. "They serve a bouillabaisse here that'll knock your socks off."

But they didn't end up eating bouillabaisse.

"You order for me," Marlo said when the time came. "I'm sick of making decisions." She was enjoying the view out the tinted window, enjoying the crisp white tablecloth and the glistening crystal. But most of all she was enjoying the company.

The waiter recommended the salmon steak, and Cal ordered it for both of them. Once they were alone again, he turned to Marlo with a searching look. "What is this?" he teased. "Do you have a split personality that only comes out after dark?"

She blinked at him, totally at sea. "I don't know what you're talking about."

He chuckled. "I saw you at work today, Marlo Santee, lady executive. I saw the tigress in you." He glanced around the room. "Where do you hide it? I want to make sure I don't have to tangle with that animal."

She flushed, half indignant, half proud. "You're exaggerating."

He shrugged dismissively. "Maybe so. But tell me, did you win?"

She realized he was referring to the meeting with Mr. Grayson and the copywriters. "I'm not sure who won, but I think I kept myself afloat for a few more days." She sighed, leaning back in her chair. "It's not easy, you know. I have to put up a fight every time I turn around."

He raised his glass of wine and studied it. "Why don't you quit?"

She stared at him as though she might not have heard correctly. "What?"

"Quit. Get a job you like better."

He might as well suggest that she give up breathing. "But I love my job."

"You love the fighting?" he asked, squinting against the glare of the sunset.

"No, of course not. But I love creating ad campaigns." She frowned, wondering at the misty hint of emotion in his smoky blue eyes. What was he thinking? She had a feeling he was testing her, prodding, waiting for results—and that he hadn't much liked the results he'd received so far.

"What drives you, Marlo?" he asked quietly. "Why is it so important to win?"

That he, of all people, should ask her that! He'd been a winner all his life. He might only be a cowboy, but she knew without having to be told that he was a good one—that he would be good at anything he tried to do. The evidence shaded every movement he made. His confidence, his assured masculinity, his fearless adaptability all told the tale. Did he think it was really so easy for everyone else?

Well, she had news for him. It wasn't. Losing was painful, and she'd had her share of pain. It was a feeling she didn't want to have again.

"It's fun to win," she said glibly. "It's not fun to lose."

He made no further comment, but she knew he wasn't buying her explanation. She could see it in his eyes as he looked at her. He liked her. She could see that, too. He wanted her and she glowed under the strength of his growing desire. But tangled with that was still the wariness.

"Cal," she said tentatively, "I don't know quite how to say this so you won't take offense. But I think we ought not to do things at work that show, well, that we're dating."

"You ashamed to be seen with me?" he asked bluntly.

She couldn't keep back a laugh. "Quite the opposite, in fact." Tilting her head to the side, she observed him playfully. "Don't you know you're the talk of the office? Every woman in the place is drooling over you."

He moved uncomfortably. "Just my natural cowboy appeal," he muttered, but she could tell he was embarrassed.

"It isn't that I don't want to be seen with you. It's just that I'm sort of fighting for my life at Grayson's. If this thing doesn't go, I'm probably finished. Anything that tends to work against me could scuttle the project. And having it known that I'm dating my star model might... Oh, you know what I mean." She stared miserably into her salad. "I just don't want to give anyone any ammunition against me. Not now while everything is so precarious."

He didn't reply, and she finally looked up to see him eating as though she hadn't spoken. But he'd heard. She knew he'd heard.

Dinner was wonderful. They talked and laughed and filled themselves with good food, then left the restaurant to walk on the beach in the moonlight. They'd planned a quiet stroll, but by the time they got out on the sand, Marlo's shoes in Cal's back pockets, the beach was crowded with people.

"What's going on?" Marlo asked, watching the cars drive up and warmly dressed people, most carrying plastic pails, descend upon the shoreline.

"Looks like the grunion are running," Cal said.

"Grunion?" She wrinkled her nose. "What are grunion?"

His teeth flashed in the dark. "You're not from around here, are you, lady? Haven't you ever heard of grunion?"

She shook her head. "I don't think so."

"Well, you're probably going to see some tonight."

They walked on, dodging a couple of children who were careering around like bumper cars. "What exactly are grunion?" she asked at last.

"Damned if I know," Cal answered with a smile in his voice, "but they seem to run a lot."

"What are grunion?" A tiny woman with a large plastic pail stopped to enlighten them. "Little silver fish about half a foot long. Good eating. They come up at certain tides to spawn. Male and female come out of the water together, lay and fertilize the eggs, then go back on the next wave. It all takes about fifteen seconds. We catch 'em while we can."

"Thank you," Marlo began, but the woman was hurrying down to the tide line to get into position for the hunt. "Now why didn't you know that?" she teased Cal.

"Cowboys don't do much fishing," he grumped. "But I do know you have to catch them with your bare hands. Nets are illegal." He took her arm. "Want to give it a try?"

A wave swept up across the sand, and suddenly the shore was alive with a thousand wriggling silver bodies. Amid shouts of excitement, the hordes on the beach swooped down and reached for the little fish.

"Oh, no," Marlo objected, holding back. "The poor things!"

Cal pulled her close. "This from a woman who just put away a salmon steak, not to mention a dozen or so shrimp in her appetizer. Did you shed a tear for them?"

She knew he had her, but she wasn't about to admit it. "Certainly," she said primly. "Just like the Mock Turtle did in *Alice's Adventures in Wonderland.*"

He laughed and they walked on, eventually leaving the crowds of fishermen behind. "How's your sunburn?" he asked as they found their own isolated section of beach.

Marlo felt her heartbeat begin to accelerate. "Fine," she said, and it was almost true.

He stopped and lightly kissed one of her shoulders, then the other. "Not fine enough," he said softly. "Not yet."

She knew what he meant and that he was doing this for her, but her heart cried out in anguish. She wanted him in her bed. She wanted his body, hard and warm, to hold hers through the night. Remembering her dream, she shuddered slightly, and he pulled her into his arms, taking her mouth with his own, kissing her, enticing her, his arms so gentle, his mouth so demanding that she knew the meaning of fire and ice.

His tongue stabbed into the sweet warmth of her mouth, plundering as though he would devour her, and she reached up to dig her fingers into this thick hair, pulling him harder against her, begging for more.

"Your sunburn . . ." he began hoarsely.

"No!" she rasped fiercely, and her hands slid up under his shirt. His muscular chest was smooth and hot, just as she'd known it would be. She ran her hands over his flesh hungrily, wanting him with an urgency that took her breath away. She'd never felt such thrilling need.

"Love me, Cal," she whispered.

"I'm going to love you, boss lady," he groaned into the curve of her neck. Her blouse had come open, and he reached inside to cup a breast, pulling it out of the lacy bra she wore, curling a finger about the hard nipple. "I'm going to love you till you cry for mercy," he vowed, tasting her neck with tiny, wild bites. "If it weren't for the damned grunion bringing all these people to the beach, I'd do it right here, right now."

She sighed as a group of grunion hunters came closer, their pails clanging. With effort they both restrained the growing fever they'd ignited. She closed her eyes, leaning against him. He nuzzled the silkiness of her hair and began to sing a snatch of his silly song again.

She giggled. "That awful song."

He sang another line and said, "I mean every word of it."

"It doesn't even scan."

"It doesn't have to scan. It only has to be true."

The people were getting too near. Slipping her hands from under his shirt, she quickly adjusted her own clothes. She'd never done anything like this in so public a place before, and she felt deliciously wicked.

He pulled her to him again when she was finished. "Marlo, Marlo," he whispered huskily into her hair. "You scare me."

Scare him? She was sure nothing ever scared him. She was the one who was frightened.

"I feel this way about you," he went on softly, "and we've never even made love."

His words sent a thrill through her, but she wanted to stop him, to tell him it was all right, that she was ready. She pressed against him, burying her face in the warmth of his chest, listening for his heartbeat.

He was still talking, rocking her against him as though she needed comfort. "And after we do make love," he whispered, "I have a feeling I'm not going to want to let you go."

What was he talking about? Surely not love and marriage. She closed her eyes for a moment and swallowed hard, forcing that thought away. No, nothing of the kind. So there was no reason for her heart to pound so hard. She wouldn't have to face any decisions of that nature.

She was a career woman. Her whole life was wrapped up in her work, in proving herself. That had always been her goal, and she wasn't about to give it up now.

She opened her eyes again. His own were clear and wondering. Then his hands cupped the rounded swell of her bottom, fingers digging in, pressing her into the hard curve of his hips. She felt the thrusting promise he carried, and she saw desire flare in his eyes.

She ran a tongue across her dry lips. "Possessive, are you?" The best thing to do was turn it into a joke. "Is that the way you are with all your women? If so, you must have an awfully big harem at home."

He didn't smile the way she'd expected. Instead, he turned her, and they started back across the sand. "I am possessive, Marlo," he said at last, his voice rough. "And that's what scares me."

She didn't have time to respond. A child came racing out of the water and hit her just below the knee-caps, sending her lurching despite Cal's strong arm.

A huge pair of eyes shone beneath a mop of black curly hair. "Oh, sorry, lady," the urchin said earnestly. "But look at how many I caught!"

The boy couldn't have been older than ten, and his pail was filled with silver wrigglers. He displayed them proudly. "I guess you didn't catch any, huh?" he sympathized. Then he brightened. "You want a few of mine? I've got plenty."

Marlo wanted to ruffle his wild hair, but didn't dare test his young masculine pride on such short acquaintance. Odd how much more she was noticing and liking people of the male gender these days.

"We're just watching them run," she told the boy. "But thanks anyway."

He waved and ran down the beach to join his family, carrying his pail carefully.

Marlo watched him go, feeling suddenly shy about turning back to Cal. But he didn't say anything as they continued their walk. He seemed as reluctant to explore the issues as she did.

She turned her face toward the sea, watching the moon spread its fire across the black water. Another wave brought more grunion, but not nearly as many as before. It looked as though the grunion run was winding down.

"The poor little things," Marlo repeated finally. Cal was holding her close to his side, shielding her from the cool night air. "They've just made up their minds to start a family and look what happens to them."

"That'll teach them," he answered callously. "They should have known better in the first place."

"Don't you believe in families?"

In the pale moonlight his face was stark, with shadows hiding the humor she loved so much. "To tell you the truth, the subject's never been a top contender for my attention," he told her. "I haven't given the matter a lot of thought."

He didn't want to discuss it, she realized as they reached the car and got in. In fact, he'd been reticent about anything personal from the day they'd met. Was he hiding something, or just protecting a vulnerability? She really knew nothing about him.

Nothing except that she liked his smile and the way his eyes narrowed when he drove and the low, sensual rumble of his voice when he turned to make a comment. When he looked at her, even for a flashing moment as he just had, she had the sense that he was seeing nothing but her. And when he touched her, something jolted deep, deep inside. It was wonderful to be with him. But was it enough?

That depended, she told herself sternly, on what she had in mind. As his employer for a modeling assignment, she knew more than enough about him. As a partner in a short affair as well. But for anything else, for anything meaningful or important, what she knew about him was woefully inadequate. It was time she found out a few things.

He pulled into her parking space at the apartment and turned off the engine, then shifted in his seat to look at her. "I'm not going up with you."

"You're not?" A surge of desolation swept through her. She hadn't realized how much she'd counted on his company for the night.

He shook his head. "Half the people I met today seem to live in your apartment building, or have friends who do. If you don't want people at work to know we're seeing each other..."

He was right, but she was still disappointed. She glanced at him covertly, wondering if that were the real reason, or if he were making excuses. His mercurial moods were too much for her to read. "I guess you're right," she said reluctantly. "But where will you stay?"

"I can stay with a friend."

Male, she hoped. She found herself almost asking and bit her lip just in time. "You'll need some money," she said instead. "Why don't you let me give you an advance on your salary." She began reaching for her purse, and his hand shot out, capturing her wrist.

"Marlo, Marlo," he said, bringing her hand to his mouth and kissing her palm. "You're such an innocent."

She bristled, but not for long. His warm lips sent a rush of heat through her system, and his mustache tickled a tantalizing confusion across her skin. She hadn't the slightest idea why he'd called her an innocent. She wished she could be as knowing and world-weary as she somehow imagined Cal's other women must all have been.

"Are you married, Cal?" she asked abruptly.

His head snapped up. "What?"

She stuck to her guns. "Are you married or anything like that?" She shook her head despairingly. "I really know so little about you. For all I know, you've got a wife and ten children waiting at home for you right now."

He dropped her hand and slumped down in the driver's seat, looking out the windshield. "I'm not the kind of man who spills his guts to everyone he meets," he told her gruffly. "If you want to know something about me, you'll have to ask." He paused only briefly before adding, "And no, I'm not married."

She settled back in her own seat, pulling her legs up under herself to get comfortable. "Tell me about how you grew up," she suggested eagerly. "Something about your parents."

He ran a hand through his thick, tousled hair. "You want the whole log cabin routine, do you?" But his tone was mild. "Okay. I was born in New York. I lived there until I was twelve."

That seemed impossible. "New York! But you're so Western!"

"Yup. Manhattan. Private schools, the whole bit. Then I got sick. I had some sort of upper respiratory infection they couldn't pinpoint the cause of. My mother dragged me from one specialist to another, but no one had the answer. Finally she defied everyone and took me to California, to the ranch where she'd grown up. And I never went back East."

His mother had been special to him. She could hear it in his voice. "Tell me about her," she urged.

"My mother?" Memory softened his face as he turned to her. "She had black hair, sort of like yours." He touched her hair, raking his fingers through the ebony richness of it. "And dark eyes that saw so clearly—but not into the real world. Everywhere she looked, she saw dreams."

"Is she . . . what happened to her?"

"She belonged to another age. She couldn't withstand the pressures she had to live under. Life ran over her like a steamroller."

Suddenly his mood swung again, and he grinned at her. "That couldn't ever happen to you, could it? You're much too tough."

"Tough?" she asked in surprise.

"I've seen you at work, lady. You can handle the sharks. Just don't become one of them," he added.

It occurred to Marlo later, as she was lying in bed staring into the darkness and feeling alone, that Cal had never said a word about his father. That was curious and perhaps significant. But his feelings for his mother were obvious. He'd adored her, and he'd resented the forces he felt had crushed her. Whatever they were.

And he thought Marlo was tough. She grinned wryly in the darkness. She must be putting up an awfully good front if she'd fooled Cal. In reality, her insides were jelly, shaking most of the time. She was scared to death. Couldn't he sense that? He said she scared him, but he only meant she was taking up time and energy he'd rather spend elsewhere.

She turned restlessly, tying her covers in knots. Here she was, eyes wide open, mind racing, and what she really needed was sleep. There would be more problems and decisions tomorrow, and she should be rested and ready. Instead, her mind was full of Cal.

A tiny frown furrowed her brow as she realized how much of her time was taken up with thinking of the man. Usually when she had a project pending, she was obsessed with it, and nothing could break her concentration. But not this time. She was working on the most important campaign in her life, and she was thinking about a man instead.

That had to stop, at least for the time being. Closing her eyes resolutely, she promised herself that the next day would be devoted to business.

7

SHE KEPT HER PROMISE to herself. When she woke in the
morning, she banished all thoughts of Cal from her
mind and concentrated on how she would handle the
ad presentation for Mr. Caron and his crew. The
thought of it terrified her enough to keep her occupied
until she left for the office.

She got a ride in with Mary Jane, since her car was
still in the TransUniversal Building's parking lot.
Bounding up to her floor, she felt ready for anything life
had to throw at her this morning. "Anything new?" she
asked as Jeri handed her the day's mail.

"Not really." Jeri hesitated. "Just that Ted stopped by."

Marlo sighed as she walked over to her desk. "Already? He doesn't believe in giving the other guy an
even break, does he?" She expected Jeri to meet her
smile, but for some reason her assistant was avoiding
her eyes. She plopped down in her chair. "What did he
have to say?" she asked a bit sharply.

"Oh, nothing." Jeri was a failure at hiding things.
"Just his usual venom about . . . things."

With a flash of intuition, Marlo knew exactly what
he'd come to gossip about. The whole agency probably knew by now that she had left the evening before
with her model for the Caron account. That he'd pulled
her into his arms in front of everyone. Ted had no doubt

been able to concoct some wonderful—and totally scandalous—theory as to why. She looked down at the envelopes in her hand and began to open them busily.

"Good old Ted," she said lightly. "What would we do without him to keep us on our toes?"

Jeri paused and for a moment Marlo was sure she was going to ask about Cal, about just what relationship he and Marlo had formed. "That's Ted all right," she said instead. "He keeps us on our toes, and we keep him in stitches." She brandished a small fist. "Which is just what I'd like to give him!"

Marlo smiled. Jeri was always threatening physical violence against the tall, insolent Ted, but Marlo couldn't imagine her going through with it. What she could imagine was the shocked look Ted would have on his face if someday Jeri did pop him one, and that put her in a better mood to begin work.

And work she did, shuffling papers, answering phones and making appointments, all the time trying to work up some new copy on the side, until suddenly it was noon, and Cal was leaning against her doorframe.

"Hi, there," he said, filling her office with his vibrant warmth. "Did you dream about me?"

"Not this time." She smiled at him, wondering if the bittersweet, wrenching sensation around her heart meant what she thought it might—something she didn't dare put into words. "But I'll give it a try tonight."

Two long strides was all it took for him to close the distance between them. He bent, taking her face in his hands and tipping it up. Softly he kissed her lips, then smoothed her hair away from her face. She wanted to close her eyes and drift away in his embrace.

"Don't bother dreaming tonight," he whispered, his face close to hers. "We'll let reality do the job."

The smile froze on her face. "Oh, Cal, I'm going to be busy tonight," she said, talking quickly because she knew he wasn't going to like what she had to say. "I've got dinner with Mr. Caron and his wife, and after that there's a meeting."

He straightened, his eyes mild and watchful. But his lips were still tilted in a smile. "You've got to sleep sometime," he said lightly. "Let's talk about it over lunch."

She shook her head regretfully. "I've got a lunch appointment with Mr. Grayson." She hated to see the warmth drain from his face, and impulsively she rose and reached for him. "Maybe after the meeting tonight . . ."

"Ah-hah," came a voice from the doorway. Marlo whirled to find Ted smirking there. "Planning to meet in the shadows, are you?" His eyes sparkled with intrigue. "Who are you hiding from?"

Marlo sprang away from Cal and immediately regretted it. She knew it made her look guilty. And she knew Cal had noted it, too, and hadn't liked it a bit.

"Where is Jeri?" she demanded. "She's supposed to keep unwanted visitors out."

"She wasn't at her desk. Luckily." Ted's face took on a woebegone look. "Are you implying that you don't welcome me, Marlo? That my presence is somehow a burden, an unwanted intrusion in your life, a—"

Marlo cut into the flow of his self-absorbed rhetoric. "Ted! We are having a private conversation and you're interrupting."

Cal looked slowly from Ted to Marlo and back again. His face was completely emotionless, but his knuckles were white as he gripped the brim of his Stetson. "Never mind," he said quietly. "We were finished anyway."

"Cal!" Marlo reached out to stop him, but he avoided her hand.

"See you later," he said gruffly, his eyes cold as an Arctic night. "I've got to go play pretty boy for the folks downstairs."

She watched his departure with mixed feelings. She hated to see him leave disgruntled, but it was a bit of a relief not to have to fight him—and herself—to keep her concentration on her work. Maybe it was better this way. Later, when the campaign had been formulated and was moving into production . . .

"Sorry to break into your reverie." Ted was still standing in the middle of her office. "I just thought I'd come by and see if you wanted to show me your plans for the Caron account."

"Oh, Ted, go away," she said crossly, not wanting to deal with him now. Her mind was in turmoil, and this was one day she was going to need all her wits about her. "I've got lunch with Mr. Grayson, and I'm late as it is."

She was too busy rummaging for her purse to notice the cold look that crossed the copywriter's face. "Such lofty heights for such a little bird," he said, turning to leave. "Beware of flying too high, Marlo."

THE LUNCH WITH ART GRAYSON went well, she thought. Two other account executives joined them, and they had a pleasant conversation over lobster salad and Napa Valley Pinot Blanc. She was treated as an equal by all of them, which buoyed her spirits. Then came the parting shot.

The others had been talking about a midsummer tradition, the weekend retreat at the Graysons' cabin at Lake Arrowhead. "Cabin" was perhaps a misnomer. Marlo had heard that "chalet" might better describe the classy dwelling. An invitation to the retreat was a coveted reward for a year of success.

The other two at the table were obviously sure of their reception, and they seemed to assume Marlo would be coming, too. "Be sure to bring along plenty of suntan lotion," one advised, "because we spend most of the day out on the lake."

"And don't forget your own private hangover remedy," chuckled the other. "We spend most of the night partying."

"Tell her, Art," urged the first man as they rose to leave the restaurant. "Tell her what a good time she'll have."

"Oh, I'm sure she'll have a wonderful time," Mr. Grayson said calmly. "If she comes."

The qualifying phrase sliced through her like a knife. The others noticed it, too, and there were no more words of advice on what to bring.

"But I'll be there," Marlo told herself stubbornly as she settled behind her desk again. "You just wait and see. I'll be there."

The afternoon sped by, and before Marlo knew it, it was five o'clock.

"You going to stay here all night?" Jeri asked.

"No." Marlo sighed. "I've got that dinner with the Carons tonight. You wouldn't want to stand in for me, would you?"

Jeri laughed. "Are you kidding? I'm going home to cuddle up to a warm TV. At least I don't have to talk back to it."

Marlo pushed aside her paperwork and stared at her assistant with a slight frown. She'd never known much about Jeri's private life, and come to think of it, she'd never given it much thought. She'd been so busy trying to make it in the world of advertising that her usual interest in those around her had been sidetracked. Suddenly she regretted that.

"Have you ever been married, Jeri?" she asked, almost as though she were making up for lost time.

Jeri gave a toss of her head. "No way. Are you kidding? Give up my freedom to cater to the wishes of some man? Never."

Marlo thought she detected just a bit too much vehemence. "Never?" she asked skeptically. "You've never even been tempted?"

Jeri shrugged, avoiding Marlo's eyes. "Sure I've been tempted," she said, her voice husky. "Who hasn't?" She swallowed and looked Marlo in the eye, almost defiantly. "But I got stung. The only thing in this world with an ego larger than a man's is a Persian cat, and I've already got one of those. So what else do I need?" Suddenly she was her usual bouncy self. "See you tomorrow. Do a good job of cozying up to the Caron people, and maybe they'll pay for my Western clothes." And she was gone.

Dinner with Mr. Caron and his wife went smoothly. Marlo gave them just enough information about her plans to whet their appetite, but not enough to shoot her down. Two glasses of wine left her slightly lightheaded, but she kept her meeting with the Caron brand manager anyway. And when he turned out to be a middle-aged man whose wife supposedly didn't understand him, she managed to fend off his heavy-handed passes without insulting him. It was in the middle of that meeting, held at his request in a cocktail lounge, that she began to think about Cal.

"You know, I could seal it up for you," Joe Taggert was saying blurrily, leaning close and leering. "I could make sure you got the account on every piece of electronics we carry."

Marlo nodded absently, not even listening any longer. She twirled her swizzle stick in the vodka collins she hadn't touched and saw Cal's blue eyes.

Joe went on, talking grandly of production projections and marketing studies, and Marlo stared at him, wondering how she could possibly have chosen this useless encounter over a night with Cal. Nothing was being accomplished here. She was just baby-sitting a lonely man who wanted an audience.

What was Cal doing? she wondered. "I am possessive," he'd told her the night before. "And that's what scares me."

She hadn't quite figured out what he meant by that. But he hadn't liked the fact that she was too busy to see him tonight. Tonight, when her sunburn was no longer a problem . . .

"I'm sorry, Joe," she said impulsively, reaching for her bag. "I've just remembered something. I've got to hurry home."

"What's the matter, what's the problem?" he asked, his speech getting more slurred by the moment. "What's wrong?"

"I left my microwave on," she said off the top of her head. "I've got to get back before it goes on overload and sucks in my entire kitchen."

"Oh, yeah." He stared at her for just a moment, then shook his head as though to clear it. "Sure, I know what you mean." He nodded wisely. "Those things can get mean if you don't treat them right."

"Exactly." She slid out from behind the booth. "Thanks for the lovely evening. I'll get home all right. Don't bother." She gave him a forced smile and escaped.

She raced home and with trembling fingers dialed the number Cal had given her.

"Hello?" The voice was definitely not Cal's.

"May I speak to Cal James?"

"Cal's out tonight." There was a pause. "Is that you, Janice?"

Marlo's heart splintered into a million pieces. "No, this isn't Janice."

"Oh." The voice was regretful. "Sorry. You sound so much like her."

"Will . . . do you know what time he'll be in?"

"Sorry again. May I take a message?"

"No. No message." She put the receiver back down and stared at it.

Well, what had she expected? Of course there was a Janice. There was probably a ton of them. Wonderful men like Cal didn't escape the notice of women, and every woman she knew was on the lookout for that kind of man. A real man. Her man, she thought resentfully, for that was the way she'd begun to think of him. Damn Janice, anyway.

She hadn't realized something so simple could hurt so much. Nothing had actually happened. Her voice had been mistaken for someone named Janice, someone Cal knew. And yet that tiny fact had settled a stone of dread in the pit of her stomach. She couldn't get rid of it.

Resolutely she pulled out her briefcase and got together some papers on the Caron account. She shuffled through them again and again, trying to focus, but all she could think about was Cal—Cal and Janice. Was she a blonde? A redhead, maybe? Did she love him? Had they known each other long? Was she soft and vulnerable, like Cal had said his mother was?

"Cal," she whispered, hand to her mouth, "can't you see that I'm vulnerable, too?" Much too vulnerable when it came to cowboys with searching blue eyes.

For a while she kept the hope alive that he might drop by later in the evening. But as midnight approached, she realized he wasn't coming. She went to bed alone.

The next morning was grim and overcast and fit her mood. When she first awoke, she was sure the phone would ring any moment, and he would be on the line asking again about her dreams. But as seven o'clock blended into eight, she had to face facts. He wasn't calling her.

She picked up the receiver more than once, ready to dial his friend's number, but a nagging reluctance stopped her every time. Suppose he wasn't home yet. That was something she didn't want to know.

THINGS WEREN'T ANY BETTER at work. Jeri was in an unusually foul mood, and Marlo hadn't been at her desk for more than fifteen minutes when Art Grayson called.

"You promised me some figures, Marlo," he barked. "Where are they?"

Marlo winced. She'd forgotten all about them. "Hasn't—hasn't Research gotten them to you yet?"

"It's up to you to get them to me. I want them, and I want them now." The click as he hung up rang in her ear.

Something close to panic gripped her. How could she have forgotten? She should have been up at Research all day yesterday making sure they got those statistics compiled. Now she would have to lean on them, but how could they possibly get the figures together in time to satisfy Mr. Grayson? She had no illusions that they might have finished the job without her prodding. Research just didn't respond in less than three months' time unless threatened with mass executions.

She briefed Jeri on the problem as quickly as she could, then dashed into a waiting elevator, her mind churning. At the proper floor the elevator doors ground open, and she slipped out into the hall, almost running into Cal as she turned the corner.

"Cal!" Her first burst of joy faded as she saw the reserved expression on his face. He wasn't angry, but the old wariness had returned full force, and he wasn't very glad to see her. She wanted to reach for him, to touch his hair and bring back the warm light to his eyes, but something about his coldness stopped her.

"Hello, Marlo."

Her gaze ran the length of him, taking in his crisp shirt and fresh jeans. "What are you doing here in the morning?" she asked, puzzled.

"Angel wants to rework some poses. My aim is but to oblige." His tone was bitter. Modeling wasn't his special calling; she could see that. If she only had a moment to talk to him . . . But she had to get those figures up to Art Grayson as soon as possible.

Starting to edge away, she glanced toward the door to the research department. "I've got some business to take care of, Cal," she said quickly, "but when I'm finished . . ."

One dark eyebrow rose. "Are you ever finished?" he asked impassively. "I was under the impression you were on twenty-four-hour call."

She had to explain to him, tell him what he meant to her, but not now. She just didn't have the time. Mark Steiger of Research poked his head out the door, saw her and disappeared inside again. She knew he was going to escape if she didn't hurry.

"I've got to go, Cal," she cried, starting for the door. "I'll come down to the art department as soon as I can."

She made it inside and caught Mark before he could slip out a side exit. Of course the work hadn't been completed. It hadn't even been begun. There was nothing but files of raw data.

"I can't hand Mr. Grayson this mess," she wailed. "You're going to get me kicked off the account."

"These things take time, Ms Santee." Mark was a shaggy, bespectacled man with a constant blink. "Numbers must be added and evaluated and—"

"I don't have time," Marlo fretted, looking around the office desperately. "I need something to put in front of Mr. Grayson, something concrete . . . I know!" she said, an idea finally coming to her. "I'll take your folders, and I'll take something else." She beamed triumphantly. "I'll take you."

"Me?" He clutched his coffee cup in terror.

"You." She gathered up the papers and grasped his arm, taking the coffee cup from him, setting it down on a counter and propelling him out into the hall. "You're coming to Grayson's office with me. If I can't show him results, I can show him you. And you can interpret these figures for him."

The man was actually shaking, but he calmed down once she got him into Art Grayson's office. Once he'd plunged into the substance of his work and started explaining, he regained his confidence and seemed like a new man. He told Art about the small marketing surveys Marlo had set up for him, and he interpreted the results.

"Indications are Ms Santee is on the right track," he announced. "The grandmother market is alive and kicking on this one, and they're still loyal to the old romantic concept of the West. If you can portray it effectively, you should have a winner."

He did his job well and won Marlo another few days of indulgence.

Marlo went back to her office and collapsed in her chair, letting Jeri ply her with orange juice and a damp cloth for her forehead.

"I was magnificent," she told her assistant hoarsely. "You should have been there. I said, 'Mr. Grayson, I can't give you balance sheets with results in neatly edged columns, but I can give you the man who has those balance sheets in his head. He's going to tell you what he knows.'"

Jeri gurgled with delight. "What did Mr. Grayson say to that?"

Marlo sighed. "Not a thing. He was speechless. I think he was expecting to fire me today. At least I've put that off for the time being."

Jeri went back to her desk, and Marlo sat very still. She was remembering Cal and the run-in they'd had in the corridor. She should head for the art department right away and explain to him, let him know how desperately busy she'd been, promise him anything, everything, just as long as he'd never cut her with those cold eyes again.

But she couldn't go. She was rooted to her seat. Marlo Santee, woman of the day, super executive who could handle men of all sizes, shapes and statuses, was terrified of one rough cowboy. So terrified that she couldn't bring herself to face him.

She pulled out some memos and ruffled through them, weeding out the ones that were no longer relevant and throwing them into the wastepaper basket. She was halfway through her job before she realized she was crumpling every third memo, irrespective of what the paper said. She couldn't even keep her mind on a simple job like this.

Then suddenly Cal was back again, with Jeri bobbing behind him. He stood in the doorway with legs apart, like a man in a standoff. Marlo felt a shimmering fear. He was leaving. She knew it.

"I've tried, Marlo," he said evenly. "I've given it my best shot. But it won't work."

She rose from her chair, hands gripping the edge of her desk. "What are you talking about?" she managed to ask. But she knew. If she'd only stopped to think, she would have known this was about to happen. It was inevitable. He'd never belonged here.

He came into her office, closing the door behind him, cutting Jeri off. He stood a few feet away from her, obviously not wanting to come closer. His face was a stranger's, locked and angry. "Listen, Marlo. I've been poked and prodded and stared at, like an animal in the zoo. I've had it. I quit. You're going to have to get some other clown to be my stand-in."

He was leaving. She couldn't let that happen. She tried to think of some way to keep him. Instinctively she knew that if he left now, she might never see him again. "But if you don't come in, we can't pay you—"

He cut her off with an ugly oath, eyes blazing. "You think I'm doing this for money? I don't want your damned money. You keep it."

She couldn't speak. She was afraid she might cry if she tried to. She, who never, ever cried.

"Taking orders from others is not a role I'm used to," he said by way of explanation. "It hasn't been easy. I've tried to do it for your sake. I did it as long as I could. But this is it. I've got work to do. Real work." He stared at her stricken face and swore again. "I've got to go, Marlo. If I stay, all hell's gonna break loose. I'm going."

She didn't give a thought to the Caron account, to the advertising campaign. Her heart was full of pain. He was leaving her. She couldn't bear it. "You can't go!" she said in a strangled voice. She tried to reach for him, but he seemed so far away.

"You played your cards pretty well, Marlo," he said harshly. His hand shot out and grasped the back of her neck, but his fingers weren't gentle. "You wanted me for your ads and you got me. And in the end you didn't even have to sleep with me to do it, did you?"

The words were ugly, and she cringed because the ugliness hurt. He let her go, and she felt as though she were spinning. Reaching out, she steadied herself on the edge of the desk.

"Pretty smart, boss lady," he said softly. "I guess I was wrong about you. You already are one of the sharks."

Turning on his heel, he strode from her office, leaving behind a crumpled shell of what Marlo had been just moments before.

It took her a bit of time to catch her breath. He couldn't really think that she'd been enticing him in order to get him to do the ads. Could he? She took a couple of tottering steps toward the outer office, but before she could make a real attempt to follow him, Angel burst in with Jeri right behind him.

"You seen Cal?" he asked, eyes sparkling. "Did he tell you all about it?"

"What's the matter?" she cried, knowing immediately that this had something to do with Cal's leaving. "Did something go wrong down there?"

"Yeah." Angel couldn't hold back his grin any longer. "We had a little problem down in the art department." He actually giggled, and Marlo stared at him in amazement. "That cowboy of yours just punched out Ted Hanford. Flattened him."

"What?" Her head was aching. Had he really said what she thought he had? She was vaguely aware that Jeri had gasped and then run for the elevator, but she didn't pay any attention. She had to know about Cal. "Tell me what happened."

"It was beautiful. You should've seen it. He's got a mean left hook, that boy." Angel demonstrated, jabbing into the empty air. "Ted came sniffing around, making trouble as usual. He got on Cal's nerves one too many times—I think he said something about you, in fact—and Cal got him. Pow." He made another jab with his fist. "Ted must have been two feet off the floor. He sailed through the air so pretty." He shook his head, remembering. "You should've been there."

She wished she had been—to stop it. Somehow she had a feeling that hitting Ted had been a substitute for lashing out at her. She was the one he was really angry at. She was the one who'd coaxed him from his ranch to sit on a stool and have people draw pictures of him. He had a right to complain.

"Well, I doubt if he'll be back today," Angel was saying. "And when he does come back..." He looked at Marlo, frowning a little. "I like the guy. But he's no model. In fact, he's just not very cooperative. Maybe if you could come down and stay next time... You seem to have a calming effect on him, you know what I mean?"

As though he were a wild beast to be tamed. And wasn't he? She'd taken a man who lived wild and free and asked him to act like a lapdog. He couldn't do it. She'd been a fool to ask him to.

"Could you do that?" Angel was asking again. "If he comes back, I mean."

Marlo nodded vacantly, agreeing to anything, absorbing almost nothing. She was numb. She showed Angel out of her office, closed the door and dropped into her chair, her head in her hands. Cal was gone.

She wasn't sure how long she sat there, but it seemed like forever. When Jeri poked her head in the door, it was about one o'clock in the afternoon.

"Are you all right?" Jeri asked.

"Of course I'm all right." But she knew how strained she must appear. She forced herself to sit up and tried to smile. "I suppose I should go and see how Ted is," she began, but Jeri broke in.

"Don't bother. I've seen him." Her grin was lopsided. "One side of his face has changed shape, but his mouth is still working just fine."

"I'm sure it is," Marlo replied. "Nothing short of a head transplant would stop that man from talking." She moved some papers vaguely from one pile on her desk to another.

"Why don't you go home?" Jeri said abruptly. "Take a nap or something. You look beat."

"Home?" Marlo shook her head. "I've got to work on the Caron account."

Jeri came close, hands on hips, staring down at her. "Your model on the Caron account has just quit. Or didn't that sink in?"

"You, too?" Marlo asked, gazing up at Jeri. "Do I really come across as a shark? Does everyone think business is all I care for?"

Jeri grimaced. "I don't know what you're talking about. I only know that we're in trouble here again. And that you're not dealing with it."

Marlo closed her eyes. Jeri was right. She had to get her mind back on the real issue. It was sink or swim, and she was about to be hit by a tidal wave. "Has it ever occurred to you," she said slowly, eyes narrowing, "that

every failure I've had since I came here has had something to do with Ted Hanford?''

To her surprise Jeri's gaze wavered. ''What do you
want?'' she asked. ''He's after your job. He always has
been. You can't blame him for trying.''

This from the woman who'd so often threatened to
tear his heart out with her bare hands! Marlo frowned
thoughtfully, about to ask what Jeri knew that she
didn't, but the telephone rang at that very moment, and
Jeri seemed vastly relieved to have an excuse to escape.

The afternoon loomed long and deadly in front of
Marlo. There were things to be dealt with, things Cal
had said, things she was feeling, but she held them at
bay, saving them for later when she could be alone. For
now there was always work.

8

IT WAS A RELIEF to get home to her own apartment. She closed the door and sank onto her couch, letting the day's pain ebb from her body. Cal was gone. But life would go on. After all, only a few days before she hadn't even known he existed.

She ate a lonely dinner of a simple green salad and eyed the telephone a lot. Somewhere at the other end of the wire was Cal. Why didn't he call? Surely he was going to discuss this more fully.

Finally she couldn't stand the suspense. She dialed the number where he'd been staying. She would insist he come by for a full discussion on the unfounded charges he'd made against her. She'd say he owed her at least that much. They'd clear the air. She'd convince him. Of what? Anything, everything. She wanted him back. But the telephone rang and rang and no one answered. Not even to ask if Janice was calling.

Janice. Who could she be? Theories tortured Marlo until she threw a pillow at the telephone and turned on the television. It was getting late, and there was a wonderful old film on. The heroine had a career in the fashion industry. The hero was a European count who needed a full-time wife.

"I'll think of you when apple blossoms fill the air," the count said sadly, preparing to leave without her.

"Fresh and eager, they'll remind me of you. And when they fall to the ground, their lovely pale petals will mingle with my tears...."

Of course the American girl gave up her career and ran off to join the high life of Europe. She was no fool. Who wanted to work all day when there was all that fabulous wealth to roll around in?

Was that what she should do? Marlo wondered. She could let herself be fired. Or, better yet, she could quit. Would that make Cal happy?

But that only worked when you were in love and ready to get married. There had been no talk of love. And no one had even thought of marriage. Had they?

Marlo switched off the old movie and stared at the darkened screen. Just what had her motives been? She'd desperately needed a model, and Cal had fallen into her lap, albeit reluctantly. She'd been prepared to do almost anything to snare him. She'd even told him so.

But it wasn't really like that, a part of her cried. From the very beginning there'd been much, much more. She'd responded to Cal, opened to him as she never had to any other man in her life. So why had he gone away? Why had he left her?

She closed her eyes and pressed her hands to her face, but the memories she hated came anyway. She'd been thirteen when her father had left. His betrayal had bewildered her at the time. He'd kept in touch with occasional letters and phone calls, but to all intents and purposes he was not a real part of her life from then on. And at the same time he was the major influence. Even now she couldn't think of him without pain.

Her mother had been devastated. At first she'd collapsed completely, spending days in bed, leaving the running of the house to Marlo. Then she'd emerged from the bedroom full of plans to get him back.

"Do you think, Marlo, if I dyed my hair red... Marlo, what if I got a job at that new restaurant on Duquane? Do you think your daddy would come to see... Maybe if I lose ten pounds..."

Those hopes faded, and then all she had left was little Marlo. "Write to your father, Marlo," she'd say. "Tell him about those good grades you're getting in science."

Marlo dutifully wrote. And she began working harder at school, providing new triumphs to tell him about. Her mother never put it into words, but she knew this was the only way left that they might win him back. Maybe, if she were good enough, maybe, if she were successful enough, he would be proud, and he would come home again.

"Dear Daddy," she would write hopefully. "How are you? We are fine. I won the ninth grade essay contest. My topic was 'International Brotherhood in a Shrinking World.'" Or "I'm going to be Clara in our school's production of *The Nutcracker*. Remember when you took me downtown to see it that Christmas? You said it was your favorite. We're doing it the Friday before Christmas. Are you going to be busy that day?" Or "I made the varsity volleyball team. We're playing our first game in Ellensburg. That's pretty close to where you live now, isn't it?"

He never came. There was always some reason why he just couldn't make it. But she never stopped trying.

"Even now," she whispered to herself, rising from the couch and moving toward the kitchen, "I'm still trying. Still begging Daddy to notice me."

Her father had died a few years ago, and her mother was living a quiet life in a Chicago suburb. There was no longer any reason to work so hard for approval. So why did she do it?

She put the kettle on for tea and stared at the gas flame. She knew she'd been using Art Grayson as a substitute for her father, that she'd been desperate for his approval, as though that could somehow win her father's love. A futile struggle. Ridiculous. But it was one thing to know that intellectually, to tell herself she was following a feather in the wind. It was another to convince her emotions. No matter how she analyzed her motives, she couldn't hold back the feelings. They were there, and they drove her on.

She poured the boiling water into her teapot and watched the curls of steam reach into the air. It was happening again. Her first impulse was to do something to show Cal she was worthy of him. What a senseless effort that would be. She could work herself into a vice presidency, and he wouldn't care. He wouldn't raise an eyebrow. He'd be out riding free on his range somewhere, not even thinking of her. What did her kind of success mean to him?

He'd called her a shark. She was hardly that. There was no shark in her at all—more like a goldfish trying to swim through a terrifying maze of doubt and fear. And tonight she could see nothing but dead ends. She glowered at the tea in disgust, threw it into the sink and went to bed.

"GOOD MORNING," JERI SAID as Marlo walked in the next morning. "Do we or don't we have him back?"

Marlo threw her assistant a baleful glance and went on into her own office, tossing her briefcase onto a chair. "If you're talking about California James, I haven't heard from him," she admitted as Jeri followed her in.

"Well, what are we going to do?" Jeri demanded.

Marlo held her chin high. "We're going to go on with the ad campaign just as we'd planned."

Jeri looked at Marlo as though she were afraid her boss had lost some nuts and bolts. "Wake up and smell the coffee, Marlo," she cried. "He's gone!"

Marlo tried not to wince at her words. "I know he's gone, Jeri," she replied evenly. "But we've got the sketches. Maybe he'll have second thoughts and show up for the shoot. We'll do the presentation with the sketches and continue on the assumption that he'll show."

"And if he doesn't?"

She shrugged, trying to pretend a coolness she didn't feel. "We'll find somebody else to take his place." She saw the storm in Jeri's eyes and added quickly, "Maybe we'll use Ted. Why not? He's getting pretty wild and woolly these days, taking on Cal and all."

A shadow fell across the doorway. "Did I hear my name being bandied about?" Ted came into the office with his usual sardonic smirk. The only evidence of his recent encounter with Cal's fist was a slightly smudged look to his right eye.

"You look a trifle used, Ted," Marlo said dryly. "Does it hurt?"

"Only when I see," he replied casually. "It's actually of little consequence."

"Ah-hah." Marlo nodded wisely. "A badge of honor, perhaps, like a dueling scar?"

"Something like that," he murmured, eyeing Jeri, who had suddenly become very busy with the papers on Marlo's desk. "Actually," he said to Marlo, "I was hoping you could give me Billy the Kid's schedule for the day. I want to make sure I avoid him."

Marlo couldn't hold back a smile. "Billy the Kid won't be riding our way for a while. But I'm planning to take karate lessons soon, so watch out."

Ted looked pained. "Another female combatant. I'll really be in trouble if the two of you join forces." He glanced at Jeri again. "What? No mocking laughter at my plight? No threats to make my eyes a matching pair again by blackening the good one?"

Jeri's usually bright eyes were dull and haunted as she glanced at Ted and then turned to Marlo. "Shall I run down and see how Angel is coming on the comprehensives?" she asked, deliberately turning her back on the copywriter.

"Sure, if you want to."

Jeri left the office, and Marlo and Ted looked at each other in surprise.

Ted was almost woebegone. "I like her much better when she hates me than when she doesn't seem to know I exist. It's lonely being ignored."

"Don't worry, Ted," Marlo assured him. "I still hate you. You're not forgotten."

"Thank God." It sounded heartfelt. "I don't suppose you hate me enough to let me see your copy on the Caron ad?"

Marlo hesitated. Ted was a strange one. She didn't really hate him, although she was sure he had a hand in most of what went wrong for her. But every machination he performed was done in such an impersonal way that she sometimes wondered if she were really meant to take offense. His antics were like moves in a chess game, saved from seeing evil by his ever-present sense of humor.

She was tempted for a moment to go ahead and let him see, but then she remembered the time he had brought the people from the Vege-max Burgers account into the Steer and Stein to see her eating a thick, juicy steak. She'd just spent a week taking them around to every vegetarian restaurant in town and had sneaked out to enjoy a solid meal on the sly. How he'd known she was there she never found out, but the Vege-max people had marched right back to Mr. Grayson and demanded she be taken off their account. No, Ted was not to be trusted.

"Not quite, Ted. My instinct for self-preservation is too strong for that."

"Tsk, tsk, such a Darwinian phobia. Don't you trust me, Marlo?"

"Not a bit. You believe a little too strongly that the end justifies the means."

He gave her an outraged stare. "Not at all. I believe that the Ferrari justifies the means. And the penthouse apartment, etcetera. That's quite a different thing, you know."

"Is it?" She shook her head in surrender. "I hope you make vice president one of these days, Ted. Then maybe you can relax."

"Never." The smile he threw her as he left was quite genuine, one of the most open she'd ever seen on his face, and it stunned her to realize he looked almost nice.

She turned back to her work and tried to make herself care about it. The tiny forlorn hope that Cal would call got dimmer as the day progressed. He'd had twenty-four hours to cool off. Shouldn't he call? And how were they going to let him know about the shoot if they didn't know how to reach him? She had Jeri try all the Jameses in the Antelope Valley phone book, and she herself kept dialing the number of his friend, but nothing turned up a clue.

"You have a nice weekend," Jeri said at the end of the working day. She paused at the door of Marlo's office. "No new ideas?"

Marlo shook her head. The fight seemed to have drained out of her in the past half hour or so. Things seemed a bit hopeless.

Jeri took a deep breath, let it out and moved impatiently. "I know," she said at last. "Why don't I get out my Western duds and head for Phoenix, like we planned. I could still hit some rodeo events. . . ."

"No." Marlo shook her head sadly. "Thanks, Jeri, but no." She fidgeted restlessly. "He'll come for the shoot. I know he will."

Jeri gave a snort of annoyance. "Then you've got a hell of a lot more faith in men than I have," she said harshly before turning on her heel and striding toward the elevator.

Marlo left soon afterward, driving her car slowly down Wilshire. The weather had turned hot, and the clouds of yesterday had been swept out to sea by Santa Ana winds blowing off the desert. Even late in the afternoon the sun shone so brightly it almost hurt, and everything she touched seemed to sizzle.

She passed the block where she'd found Cal. It seemed so long ago now, but it had only been a few days. Strange how time could stretch and condense at will.

She turned the air conditioner on in her apartment, but it didn't do much to cool things off, so she left her door open. That turned out to be a mistake. It was a clear invitation for visitors.

"Yoo-hoo." Mary Jane knocked, then stepped in before Marlo had a chance to stop her. "You busy tonight?"

Marlo thought fast for an excuse to avoid whatever Mary Jane might have in mind. "Well, actually—"

"Cuz me and a couple of girlfriends from Accounting are going to catch a movie in Hollywood. You ought to come. It'll be fun."

Marlo could read the sympathy on Mary Jane's face. She knew Cal was gone and she wanted to help, which was very nice of her, but hardly necessary. "Thanks, Mary Jane, but I think I'll stay home and wash my hair."

Mary Jane tossed her long blond locks. "Suit yourself. But you should come along. After the show we're going to try out this cute little place in Venice one of the girls heard about. They've got male exotic dancers." She giggled. "Let me know if you change your mind."

Male exotic dancers would not cure what ailed Marlo. But there were worse things. Mary Jane had barely disappeared when Peter arrived in the open doorway.

"Hey, Marlo, it's been so long!"

"Has it?"

"Sure. Why don't you come dancing with me tonight? It'll take your mind off things."

"Things?" She stared at him apprehensively. "What things?"

"Hey, it's obvious you're sad because you and your cowboy just split up. No big deal." His grin was puppy-dog silly. "Say, that was just about the shortest romance on record, wasn't it?"

Marlo sighed. It was one thing that Mary Jane knew all about Cal, but where on earth had Peter got his inside information? "Where did you hear that?" she asked.

He gestured grandly. "Around. Everybody knows."

All of a sudden she began to laugh. "Everybody knows? Is that the way things are here in Swinging Singles Land? All the annoyances of a small town without the conveniences."

Her laughter ended in hiccups, and she went into the kitchen to get a drink of water to calm them. Peter followed her, coming up behind her as she reached for a glass from the cabinet.

"Listen, Marlo," he said, in what he probably thought was a seductive voice, "who needs that dusty old cowboy, anyway? There are plenty of men around ready to take his place."

She jumped when she felt his hand on her shoulder. "Peter!"

Before she could stop him, he'd pulled her to him in an awkward embrace and planted a quick wet kiss on her mouth.

"I'll bet he can't do anything I can't do," Peter proclaimed, still holding her. "Just give me a chance, Marlo. I'll show you."

His face was so earnest, and despite his brave words there was nothing sexually threatening about Peter. He was still a puppy. Gently she disentangled herself from his arms. "Oh, Peter," she said rather fondly, "you know, you really are sweet in a sort of demented way."

"I'm not sweet!" he protested indignantly.

"Yes, you are." She patted his cheek and turned to fill her glass with water. "But you're not my type."

"Maybe not," he said sulkily, "but I'm here."

She closed her eyes and steadied herself. That one had hurt. "But not for long," she said cheerfully as she turned back. "There's the door. Please use it."

He did, but he grumbled all the way. "I'm going out with friends," he told her as he left, "but I'll check on you when we get back. Maybe you'll change your mind."

"Oh, don't, Peter."

"I will," he said stubbornly. "I'll drop by about ten."

"I don't answer my door after dark," she told him. "And I definitely don't open to strange men."

"I'm not strange."

She shook her head. "You will be after dark. I won't know you. So please—*please!*—don't bother to drop by."

She closed the door when he had finally gone and let the air conditioner try to bring the room to a livable temperature. Then she began the hopeless task of trying to find something to do with her evening that wouldn't give her time to think.

Reading was out. The television screen was a blur. She'd sent away every friend in the building. What was there left to do but wash her hair, just as she'd told Mary Jane she was going to do?

She took a shower, letting the water run over her until she felt almost ready to sprout scales. Then she emerged from the bathroom in her terry-cloth robe with a towel wrapped around her soggy hair and started sorting through her record and tape collection, hoping to find something that would fit her mood.

She heard voices in the courtyard. It sounded as though Peter and his friends had returned already. She hoped he'd forgotten about his promise to look in on her. Listening carefully to the fading voices, she decided she was in luck. So when the knock came on her door, every nerve in her body quivered in surprise.

She sighed. Not only did Peter not take hints, he didn't even take being hit on the head with a hammer. What was it going to take to convince him she had no interest in him?

"Forget it, Peter," she called. "I'm not opening the door. I told you I wouldn't let you in tonight."

There was a pause. She waited for Peter to say something. Talking was his specialty. But then the knock came again, harder this time, with an insistence that chilled her just a little.

"Peter?" she asked, her heart beginning to pound. "Is that you?" There was still no answer, and for the first time she wished she'd had a peephole installed in her solid wooden door. But there was something about that knock... Throwing caution to the winds, she did something she'd always promised herself she'd never do—she opened her door, late at night, not knowing who was on the other side, with only a flimsy chain to protect her.

"Cal." She stared at him over the strained length of brass chain.

"Let me in, Marlo," he said calmly. "I'd like to talk to you."

Her fingers were shaking as she undid the chain. He walked in slowly, looking around the apartment as though it had been a long time since he'd been there.

He was dressed very differently from the roughrider image he'd been projecting for her all week. Instead of the usual plaid shirt and jeans, he wore dark slacks and a black, short-sleeved jersey shirt that clung to the contours of his wide chest, emphasizing the swell of his muscular form in a way that was suddenly very threatening. His hair looked as though he'd recently been in a high wind, and his eyes were wild and smoky with some emotion she was afraid to examine too closely.

"I thought you'd be back on your ranch by now," she said nervously, trying to smile. "I thought you'd have forgotten all about me."

He looked at her for a long moment, as though he'd missed the sight of her face. Then, without speaking, he began to move toward her.

She stood her ground, blinking rapidly, an exquisite excitement cascading across her skin, quickening her heartbeat and sending her pulse racing. Moving with the grace of a cat, he stepped forward and pulled the towel from her head. Her wet hair flew about her face in a soggy veil, and she shook it back, away from her eyes, so that she could watch him. His hands cupped her face, and he gave her a quick hard kiss on the lips.

"I can't seem to forget you, no matter how I try," he said, and he didn't sound happy about it. "I told you from the first that I didn't want to get involved with you. But you couldn't leave well enough alone." He kissed her quickly again. "And now neither can I."

She couldn't speak. Her heart was full. The Caron account was the furthest thing from her mind.

"You're a slick, ambitious city girl," he lectured sternly, "and I'm a country rancher. We don't belong together."

"Opposites attract," she murmured.

"They may attract," he said gruffly, "but they can also destroy each other. You've been messing up my mind ever since the day we met. I'm just about messed up for good. Did you know that?"

She tried to laugh, to pretend he was joking, but the sound came out strained and false.

He let go of her and swung away, pacing the floor. "I mean, no one else has ever got me to dress up and pose like a monkey on a string. No one else has ever talked me into taking orders from every jerk who walks in the door. I'm not used to it." He whirled and glared at her. "I just reached the boiling point, Marlo. I couldn't take it anymore, and I had to get out of there."

"I know." She reached for him. "I'm sorry, I should never have expected you—"

"Don't you be sorry." She was in his arms again, and he was holding her close to his chest. "You're just doing what you have to do. It's me. I'm too ornery for the job." He smoothed her wet hair away from her face. "I'm the one who's sorry."

She reached up to touch his cheek, and he kissed the palm of her hand. "I'll do your damned shoot," he growled. "Just as long as you don't make me sit for any more drawing sessions with idiots jabbering away in the background."

She linked her arms behind his head and pressed herself to him. "I won't *make* you do anything, cowboy," she whispered happily. "You set the rules from now on. Just don't leave me like that again."

He didn't answer with words. One hand began to pull gently at the collar of her robe, and she threw her head back, luxuriating in the glow she felt where he touched her skin. His hand slipped beneath the fabric of the robe, thumb high on her neck, fingers curling around her shoulder. A look almost of pain swept over his hard face. "I want to make love to you, Marlo. But I've got to be honest. I wish I didn't. I wish I could walk away and never think of you again. I didn't want this."

"I know."

"Make love with me, beautiful lady. And then maybe it will all be over. Maybe I'll be able to get you out of my system."

"Cal . . ."

"I don't want to talk anymore, Marlo," he said huskily. "I want to make love. I want to bury myself in your ebony hair, I want to feel your long legs wrap around me, I want to make you feel so good, so good . . ."

She shivered at the intensity of his words. He bent his face to the bare skin he'd exposed, and she felt his tongue tasting, felt his teeth rasp against the jutting line of her collarbone. She was aroused as she'd never been before. Had she ever wanted a man the way she wanted him?

No. Never. She knew instinctively that he would be a lover she would never forget—could never equal again. Did she dare set a standard like that?

Yes. She would dare. She would take him and love him and maybe die a little in the process. But he would be hers for that brief shining moment. There was a strong drive in her that wanted that, needed it so badly. . .

"Oh, Cal," she said, gasping, as his hands worked across her shoulders, his mouth explored her skin. "You scare me," she whispered. Her knees were getting weak, and she was afraid she would have to lean against him to stay upright.

He touched her wet hair. "Don't be frightened." His hand cupped the back of her head and his voice lowered. "I would never, never hurt you," he groaned, burying his lips in the pulse at the base of her throat.

He didn't understand. She knew he wouldn't hurt her. Not physically. But there was other pain that was infinitely worse. That was what she dreaded.

His warm breath curled against her skin, his hard fingers stroking her sensitive softness. Everything was conspiring in her seduction, and she knew it was working. She could feel herself weakening with a delicious lethargy.

He reached out slowly with both hands, pulling her robe away from her. She couldn't move, couldn't speak.

"Oh, God, Marlo," he said with a gasp as he swept the cloth away, revealing her body, naked except for her tiny blue panties.

She couldn't breathe. Her breasts felt heavy and swollen, as though her sexuality were throbbing, ripe, ready to be taken. There was a pulsating ache beginning just below her navel and spreading down to her legs. She closed her eyes, feeling the touch of his gaze.

"I've lain awake for nights imagining this," he growled, his voice gravelly with anger and passion. "We're going to be so good together."

She started to speak, to protest, but his mouth closed on hers, and the only sound she made was a whimper of longing, of need. She found herself taking from him as greedily as he was taking from her. His lips devoured her, his tongue entering and claiming possession. She felt the scrape of his teeth against her lip, but she noticed no pain, only a thirsty passion to have him all, to take him in and consume him, make him part of her, hold him hard and tight and never let him go.

The frenzy that overcame her went beyond desire. There was a thrill to it, a sense of power and release from inhibition. She knew what she wanted now. There were no more doubts, only a single-minded obsession to have him, to have him all.

His hands slid down her naked curves and hooked beneath the flimsy nylon of her panties, pushing them away. He cupped her buttocks, kneading the flesh in a tantalizing rhythmic stroke. She gasped and threw back her head, inviting his mouth to explore her breasts, digging her fingers into his thick hair and pulling him harder against her once he'd begun.

There was a wildness raging in her, much wilder than the Santa Ana wind blowing outside. They were both caught in it, turning and twisting in a tumultuous, spinning storm that sent them high above reality. They were different now, two forces of nature, wild and free and completely without restraint.

She tugged at his shirt, impatient to feel more of him, but he didn't help her. He was intent on her, his mouth evoking exquisite pleasure, his hands searching out the most sensitive areas of her response. When he straightened, his belt buckle was cold and hard against her hot skin, and she cried out in frustration, wanting to feel him as naked as she was. Without thinking, she plunged her hands under his belt, reaching for the throbbing mystery that would soon possess her.

He groaned and quickly helped her undress him. Somehow they found their way to her bed. His lean body slid along hers deliciously, and then she was whispering for him, crying for him, demanding him, and he surged inside, his breath hot and labored in her ear, and she was delirious, crying out his name, digging her nails into his back, climbing peak after peak until he drove her to the very apex of wonder.

9

THEY LAY STILL, bodies tangled in a hopeless puzzle. What a ride it had been! Marlo had never, ever experienced anything like it before. She'd never known there could be such intensity, such absolute need, that she could lose herself so in loving desire. But it didn't stand alone, she knew. It was very much tied in with the man who'd created it.

How long had she loved him? Not from the very first, surely. But perhaps from the night he'd come home with her and eased her sunburn pain. Absolutely by the next morning when he'd interrupted her dream. Why had she tried to hide it?

She opened her eyes and found herself looking into the curve of his shoulder. Reaching slowly, she touched the soft hairs at the back of his neck, letting the prickly ends tickle her palm. *I love you, Cal*, she thought. But she wasn't ready to say it aloud. *I love you so very much.* She'd never told that to a man. She'd never felt it.

He turned his head to face her. His hand reached out and took a strand of her hair, curling it around his finger. "Who the hell is Peter?" was the first thing he said.

She blinked, then decided he deserved a little teasing. "Just a friend," she replied with a secret smile.

He rose on his elbow and glared at her. "Lose him," he ordered shortly. "And don't you ever open your door at night like that again."

She ran her fingers lightly down his tanned back. "If I hadn't opened my door, you wouldn't be here now."

"That's what you think." He nuzzled the side of her neck, taking in the scent of her skin as though she were an exotic perfume. "I'd have taken the place apart brick by brick to get in here."

She hid her grin against his shoulder. "Probably so. You had a goal, didn't you." She didn't know exactly why she was so confident, but she was. He'd come into her apartment insisting he wanted to get her out of his system. But they'd just made beautiful, glorious love, and he wasn't going to leave her. Not after this. She bit her lip, then asked slyly, "Well, did you get me out of your mind? Are you all over me now?"

There was a long pause, then he flopped back on the pillow. "That's another mark against you," he mocked. "You've turned me into a liar." Reaching out, he pulled her on top of him. "Lady, I'm afraid I'll never be over you."

She trembled at the importance of what he was saying. It scared her to think about it. "And do you still think I'm a shark?" Her tone was light, but he must know how the remark had hurt. Her almost-dry hair swept over his face as she looked down into his blue eyes, wondering.

He didn't answer and she frowned. "Why were you so angry at work the other day?" she asked. "Did you really think I'd use sex to get you to do the spread?"

"Did I really say a fool thing like that?" he groaned.

"Sort of." With her finger she outlined his mustache. "What was it, Cal? Just the frustrated rage of a caged mountain lion who needed to be free again?"

He laughed. "You have romantic notions, don't you, woman?" Reaching up, he pushed her hair away from her eyes. "I've got to admit I was feeling penned in. And I wanted out of the ad campaign." He looked at her questioningly. "You heard about what happened with your friend Ted?"

She couldn't suppress a smile. "Angel is in awe of your pugilistic skill."

He winced. "That was another fool thing to do. But everything seemed to come to a head all at once, and I lost control." He touched her cheek. "Mostly it was you, though. You messed with my mind, lady. I wanted you too much." He hesitated, then continued huskily. "I needed you too much. I don't like that."

"Don't you?" All her love was in her eyes, and surely he could tell. Surely it was different now, now that she knew she loved him. He wouldn't regret what they'd become to each other. He couldn't.

Still, he hadn't said she wasn't a shark, and she knew he thought she was too concerned with advancing in her job. That was something she couldn't change. It was part of her. She would have to show him, convince him it didn't matter. That he mattered more than anything else.

The feeling was so strong she rolled away, sliding to the side of the bed to look at him, bunching the sheet up as she went. The lamp was off in the bedroom, but plenty of light came in from the hallway. His body was long and golden, a supple length of masculinity that held a coiled sense of danger, like a predatory animal at rest. He lay sprawled against the pillows, completely at peace with his nakedness. His beautiful, beautiful nakedness—the wide chest rippling with muscles and dark with hair tapering down to his taut stomach, the silky skin that burned like fire and tasted like wine, the tight knotted muscles of his hips and thighs, the stunningly variable instrument of his passion. Just looking at him made her stomach tighten, and she held her breath.

She met his eyes and found he'd been watching her and knew exactly what was going through her mind—and her body.

"Just give me a minute," he teased. "We'll do it again."

Her cheeks flared and she put her hands up to cool them. "I—I don't want . . . I didn't mean . . ."

"Sure you did." His long arm reached out, and he brushed her cheek with his hand. "You've been lusting after me from the beginning, lady, one way or another."

"Cal! How can you say such a thing?"

"Easily." His hand slipped down and yanked away the sheet she'd been using to protect herself. "Now all you need to do is admit it to yourself." He pulled her closer, his hand cupping one breast. "God, you smell good," he breathed against her neck. "Like newly mowed hay or spring flowers . . ."

She moaned and let him stir the magic again. This time there was no roughness, no impatience to be one. It was slow and loving and utterly delectable, and when it was over, she felt her love for him swelling inside until she could almost burst with it.

"All night long," he murmured as they lay back again, spent and deliciously exhausted from another bout of lovemaking. "Think you can manage it?"

She didn't have the strength to laugh. "When do we sleep?"

"Who needs sleep? We'll live on catnaps."

She smiled, eyes half closed. "'And we shall glide on serpents' scales,'" she murmured.

"No poetry. You start on poetry, I'll sing you another song."

"Thanks for the warning."

"Didn't you like my song? I made it up just for you."

"Let's put it this way: no one's perfect."

His sigh was long and sad. "And here I thought I was. Isn't that what you said?"

"Mmmm-hmmm. But I lied."

"Lie some more," he whispered, his breath stirring her drying hair.

She'd never thought she would have anything like this. Love was for movies and storybooks. Real life required strength and determination, and love only got in the way of those things. But now she realized how wrong she'd been. Now she knew that love fueled life. Without it she would wither like an uprooted flower.

What had all the turmoil been about, anyway? All the reluctance and fear? It seemed so simple now. One plus one made two.

"All night long?" he purred against her ear. "We'll never stop."

"Oh, no," she moaned. "I'll be dead."

"But in heaven."

SHE WOKE with the morning light. There was no feeling of strangeness at being in bed with Cal. She snuggled against him, feeling a comfort she'd never known before, like a kitten on a sunny windowsill.

"Are you asleep?" he whispered.

She shook her head, eyes still closed.

"I'm taking you home today."

She opened her eyes and stared at him. "Home?"

He nodded, brushing back her hair and smiling down at her love-swollen lips. "I've tried your kind of life for a whole week. How about you come and try mine for a weekend?"

"What do you mean?"

"Come with me to the ranch."

The ranch. An alien abode she'd never tried before. What would happen there? Would his people— whoever they might be—accept her? Would it be rough and foreign? Would she hate it?

"Of course I'll come."

And she would love every minute of it. It was his life, after all. How could she not love it? It was what had made him what he was. She closed her eyes again and vowed fiercely to love it almost as much as she loved him.

10

BUT GOOD INTENTIONS WERE not always enough. They got a late start, and the sun was high as they took the freeway to the Antelope Valley. As the residential sections of the Los Angeles area gave way to cactus and Joshua trees, Marlo began to get an uneasy feeling in the pit of her stomach.

She became more and more quiet as they drove farther from the sort of civilization she was used to, and Cal became more garrulous, pointing out the landmarks and pathways of his youth. She could feel his satisfaction grow. He was going home.

"How long have you had the ranch?" she asked.

"It belonged to my mother's family." He inhaled deeply, as though breathing fresh air for the first time in ages. "Actually, it's a breeding station for my main spread, which is up in Paso Robles."

"Paso Robles?" She couldn't place it in her mind.

"That's a town up the coast, about halfway to San Francisco."

"Oh." Not quite a dusty cowboy, she realized, not with two ranches to his credit. She had a feeling she was going to be in for more surprises on this visit.

They turned off the freeway and took a long, winding, two-lane road into the hills. A single line of pepper trees shaded the driveway into the ranch house.

Marlo found herself gripping the seat with both hands as they drove down it. She had no idea what to expect.

But things started well. The ranch house looked small and picturesque. "Red tile," she noted.

"Red tile," he agreed. "You may even have seen this place before. They used it as a setting in a couple of old Western movies back in the thirties and forties."

And luckily Cal's foreman took a liking to her from the beginning. As they pulled up in front of the low, Spanish-style ranch house, he came out of the shadows to greet them. He was weather-cured to an indeterminate age, somewhere between old and ageless. He wore a soiled Stetson low over his eyes and walked with a rolling gait that fairly screamed "cowboy!" When he saw Marlo getting out of the Mustang, he quickly doffed the hat and beamed at her, a wide, face-cracking smile with blue eyes sparkling in the depths of the tan wrinkles.

"Hey there, Cal. I see you got somebody with you." He waggled a finger at her and came around the car to see her better. "Hello there, pretty little lady."

At that point she wasn't sure just who he was, but she could tell by the way Cal was grinning that he was someone special. "Hello there, handsome stranger," she said happily. "Who are you?"

He stopped aghast, as though the question had never been asked of him before. "Who am I? Cal's nearest and dearest, that's all. If you don't count Aunt Emma."

Marlo responded to his warmth. "Oh, I'd never count Aunt Emma," she assured him, putting out a hand for him to shake.

"Good." He slapped his leg. "She's an ornery old cuss. Her and me, we don't see eye to eye on Cal here.

So she don't come to visit much anymore." He turned to nod approvingly at his younger friend. "I been with him since he was a toddler, one way or another. And with his mama before him. I guess you might say we've been together just about forever."

"His name's Waco," Cal told her. "I'll tell you all his secrets later."

Waco whirled to glare at Cal, but he couldn't manage it and ended up chuckling instead. "Yeah, I guess I got some good ones," he muttered as he picked up a couple of their bags and started in with them. "But don't you go shocking this pretty little lady. I don't want her to think badly of me."

They watched him disappear into the house, and Marlo turned to Cal. "Little lady," she chortled. "That's the first time I've ever been called little anything."

"All ladies are little to Waco. He's an old-fashioned guy."

"Maybe I ought to clue him in to the modern age," she said automatically, not really thinking about what she was saying, just talking to cover up her reaction to the drabness of the ranch. A dry brown area behind a fence looked as though it might once have been a lawn, but that must have been long ago. The adobe exterior of the house was patched and crumbling. Everything looked so rustic that she almost expected to find floors of hard-packed dirt inside.

But Cal hadn't noticed her disappointment in the appearance of the place. He was still reacting to her offhand comment.

"You leave Waco alone." His voice was sharp, and her head snapped up in surprise. "Let him enjoy his fantasies while he can." The harshness went out of his voice, and he put an arm around her shoulders, leading her into the house, but his words still stung. "You keep your city opinions for your city friends. People who stay out here usually do so to avoid that kind of thing."

Flabbergasted, she didn't know what to say to him. She was no feminist crusader, and he knew it. What was he talking about?

But as she let him lead her into the house, she began to realize that he was as nervous about this visit as she was. He loved his ranch and wanted her to love it—he wanted it to love her—and he wanted everything to stay the way it was, all at once. Impossible, of course, but he was hoping.

The interior of the house was cool and spacious, with heavy, rough-hewn furniture and worn Navaho rugs. A huge native stone fireplace dominated the living room. There wasn't much in the way of decoration, and what there was looked like it had come from another century—oil paintings of Western scenes like those Remington once painted, copper kettles, Pueblo pottery. Marlo looked around at it all in wonder. She felt as though she'd invaded a dusty old museum in some sleepy backwater. This was nothing like what she was used to.

"Here's your room," Cal said, opening the door into a room done all in white with pink ruffles, as out of place in the house as a flamingo at a rodeo.

"My room?" Marlo looked at him questioning, the significance of what he'd just said sinking in slowly. "You mean we've each got our own room?"

Cal was more uncomfortable than she'd ever seen him before. He glanced down the hall at where Waco was turning into another doorway and told her in a hushed voice, "That doesn't mean we have to stay in them all night. But just for—"

"Appearance' sake?" She couldn't believe her ears. "Don't tell me, let me guess. Waco wouldn't approve."

She giggled with delight at the notion, and Cal turned a little red. "That's right. He wouldn't." He shrugged. "I don't see that we've got any need to upset him unnecessarily."

"California James," she whispered, coming up and standing very close. "I think you're kind of neat."

He was embarrassed, but he leaned down to kiss her. Just before his lips touched hers, Waco's voice boomed down the hall, jerking them both apart.

"Hey there, Cal! I got your stuff stowed. You gonna want lunch?"

"No, thanks. We had a late breakfast on the way."

"Okay." He bobbed his head to Marlo. "I'll go on out and see how the boys are coming with the inoculations on that bunch of steers we got in from Fort Worth last week." He said "inoculations" as if it were four or five words strung together, rather than one, then smiled as though proud of getting through it. Marlo grinned back, feeling happy and amused. But that feeling was to be short-lived.

"Come on," Cal said once they'd settled in, "I'm going to teach you to ride a horse."

Panic quivered just below her skin. "Why do we have to do that?"

He reacted as though she'd just asked what sense there was in all this bother about breathing. "Come on, Marlo. You've got to ride. Horseback is the only way you can really see this ranch."

Something told her there'd be no getting out of this one. There was a dull throbbing at her temple. A headache was threatening. She sighed. "Don't you have a jeep or something?" She peeked through the bedroom curtains at the hills. "Maybe a helicopter?"

He thought she was joking. "You're going to ride, lady." His hands swept into her thick hair, and he smiled down at her. "You'll find that out here I'm the boss."

She had no doubt about that. There was a difference about him now. It was subtle, but obvious. He was commandingly male and sure of himself in the city, but out here on his own ranch, he seemed to become positively regal, ruler of all he surveyed. And the people she saw him come in contact with, including Waco and the other hands, treated him like some sort of minor regent. Their own private sun-god.

So there was no one to save her. He got her on a horse. Luckily it was a broad-backed, placid animal that stood still as a statue, seemingly bored by it all. But she had to struggle aboard in front of a couple of ranch hands who were, she was absolutely sure, snickering at her ineptitude behind their hands, making her feel hot and red-faced before she'd even begun to ride.

"Cal! It's so far to the ground!" She was hanging on for dear life—a life she was sure was about to flash before her eyes.

Cal thought she was being ridiculous. She could see it in his face. "Willie is not going to hurt you. She's broad as a barn and just as gentle. Just let her take you. She knows where to go."

And off they went. Marlo felt every bone jolt at each step the huge animal took. She couldn't imagine how anyone might want to do this sort of thing for fun.

"Pure masochism," she grumbled to herself through clenched teeth.

Meanwhile, Cal was pointing out some of the cattle, explaining what they were breeding them for, and she was trying hard to listen. But it took too much of her energy just to hang on.

They rode past a series of low hills. "See that big boulder? I used to climb up on that and scout for rabbits when I was a kid. Rabbit stew was a common dish on our table."

The only rabbits Marlo had ever seen were the sweet, long-haired bunnies sold by pet shops at Easter time. She had a quick image of someone dropping one into a stew pot and immediately felt an unpleasant flip-flop in her stomach.

"Right over there," he went on, pointing out a flat, circular area, "used to be an Indian camp. I used to find arrowheads around there all the time."

They were climbing into a hilly region with taller chaparral. "Are there bears?" Marlo called.

"Bears? Not lately. But there are plenty of coyotes and even a puma now and then."

That was a relief anyway. Until suddenly Cal stopped their little procession with an upraised hand, swung down off his horse, flashed out his knife and then held up a decapitated rattler for her to see. The snake was about two feet long—or had been before its head had been summarily removed. "Some people think you ought to let rattlers be," he said seriously. "But with the cattle . . ." He paused, staring at her. "Hey, what's the matter? You look a little green."

"Nothing," she managed to force out, swallowing hard. "Nothing at all. Let's go." She was having trouble with her stomach, trouble with her head and now this. She only wanted him to get back in the saddle as quickly as possible so they could get this misery over with.

He took her past the little trickle of wetness he called a river to the reservoir where he'd learned how to swim, then out to the pasture to see his prize thoroughbreds. And all the while he didn't seem to notice that Marlo was hanging on by her fingernails, just barely at that.

They were passing through a green meadow when even her fingernails gave out, and she started sliding off. It was slow at first. She tried to grab on to something in the confusing array of leather to stop her slide, but everything she reached for slipped through her fingers. Slowly, very slowly, she was sliding right off Willie's back. As she went, Willie looked back at her as if to say, "Lady, if you wanted to get off, you could have told me."

She didn't cry out. She just hit the ground numbly and sat there. But Cal seemed to sense that something was wrong. He swung around and yelled, "How did you manage to do that?" as though it were the most fool thing he'd seen yet.

He could at least have asked if she were hurt. Her lower lip came out in a pout that took about twenty years off her age. "I—I—it just happened."

"It couldn't just happen," he scoffed, riding back and swinging down. "You must have stood up in the saddle and jumped."

She refused to cry, even though she felt like it. Instead, she channeled her emotions into anger. "That's exactly what I did," she declared, rising painfully from the ground without the help of his outstretched hand. "And I'm not getting back on that animal."

Cal looked more puzzled than anything else. "What? You didn't like riding?"

"No." She dusted off her bottom and began walking, wincing at the soreness in her legs. "I did not like riding," she called back over her shoulder. "But that hardly matters because I'm not going to be doing any more of it. Not ever."

"What are you doing?" He came up beside her and grabbed her wrist. "You can't walk all the way back from here."

The ranch house was in sight. She'd walked farther to catch the elevated in Chicago. "I most certainly can," she told him, eyes storm-cloud gray. "Just watch me."

In the end she did it. He tied the horses together and walked beside her, leading them. Neither one of them spoke all the way back.

By the time they reached the ranch house, Marlo's anger had diminished. She was sore and tired, but it really hadn't been that bad. Had it? She wished she could find a way to tell Cal it was all right, that she didn't hate everything. But one look at his closed face stopped her from trying.

"You go in and make yourself comfortable," he said gruffly as they approached the wide steps that led to the veranda. "I'll go tend the horses."

Watching him go, she could see his disappointment in the set of his shoulders. He loved his ranch, and he'd been ready for her to love it, too. She ached, wishing she could. But right now that was impossible. She might as well admit the truth, at least to herself. She'd never been more miserable.

Inside, the house seemed cool and comfortably shady. She rummaged through the well-stocked kitchen and came up with a carton of lemonade. She poured it into ice-filled tall glasses and carried them out into the living room. Sitting down gingerly on the couch, she leaned back against the pillows and dozed while waiting for Cal to return. The hazy golden sunshine of a late summer afternoon washed over her, and she tried not to think about what had gone wrong.

She just didn't belong here, that was all. She felt as uncomfortable as Cal had felt posing for Angel. If she'd been set down in some tropical forest and asked to enjoy a meal of grasshoppers and fried bats' wings, she might have felt the same way. But she loved Cal. So what was she going to do about it?

Cal came into the room, and she tried to smile at him, but his gaze skittered across hers and away again. "You okay?" he asked, standing awkwardly before her. "I shouldn't have made you ride so far on your first day. I'm sorry."

She couldn't have loved him more if he'd cast a handful of rubies in her lap. She wanted to jump up and throw her arms round him, but some awful reserve held her back. "No problem," she said instead, wishing she could think of a way to let him know how she felt. "I'll heal."

He grunted, reached for the lemonade and sank down in a chair facing the couch. They both sat for a long time without saying a word. This was bad, Marlo thought. There had to be some way to erase the experiences and take them back to where they'd been the night before. Then she had an idea. They did say, didn't they, that the way to a man's heart was through his stomach.

"Let me fix dinner for you," she suggested, sitting forward on the couch. "What do you love?"

He peered at her almost suspiciously. "The freezer is full of frozen dinners," he began, but she shook her head.

"I want to do it," she insisted. "You just read the paper or something."

She wanted to bound to her feet, but found rising slowly worked better on her abused body. "I'll just go make myself at home in your kitchen."

She entered that room with trepidation. Kitchens had always been somewhat outside her sphere of expertise. She wasn't sure just what she was going to do.

"What's your favorite meal?" she called to Cal.

"Chili," he answered. "With sourdough bread."

"Chili," she pondered, looking around blankly at the sparkling kitchen, at the double oven, the microwave, the food processor. "How on earth do you make it?" Opening a can was the closest she'd ever come. She didn't have a clue how to begin. Pulling open the freezer, she stared inside, as though something in the frosty depths was sure to spark an answer. But no oracle came to her rescue, so she closed it again and began opening cupboards.

She found the cookbooks, but they were filled with French and Chinese recipes, and she didn't think either one of those cultures was into chili yet.

"You need any help?" Cal was in the doorway looking incredibly handsome with his shirt unbuttoned.

"Oh, no," she answered breezily, pulling out a pan and pretending she knew what to do with it. "You just go on back and rest."

He hesitated. "The freezer and fridge are full of food," he told her. "Waco goes into town once a week and buys the place out."

"I'm sure I'll find what I need."

He left her without another word, and she stared at the empty doorway. She wanted so badly to redeem herself for the bad afternoon. If only she knew something about making chili!

Glancing out the window, she saw Waco passing by on his way to the stables. Silently she slipped out the back door and ran after him.

"Waco," she panted when she caught him, "how do you make chili?"

His expression was horrified. "You've never made chili?"

"Never. Please help me."

He must have read the desperation in her face. He gave her a fatherly grin and plunged right in. "First you get yourself a hunk of beef and cut it into chunks. Then you take a clove of garlic..." He went on, detailing quickly, and Marlo nodded, trying to commit every bit of it to memory. "You don't add beans, now," he said. "And no tomatoes, neither. Real chili doesn't take 'em. We only used stuff like that out on the trail to stretch it when we didn't have enough."

She loved to think of him on a real cattle drive. "You really did eat chili in those days?"

"Eat it? Honey, we lived on it. We slaughtered a steer first day out and had ourselves steaks half a foot thick.

Then the rest of the drive it was chili, until the beef ran out."

"And then what?"

"And then we ate our own dust." He chuckled. "Listen, if you want to make chili that will get Cal all fired up, you just follow the instructions glued to the inside of the spice shelf. I put 'em in there once for Cal's Aunt Emma when she comes, which ain't often lately. It's just like I told you, now."

She sighed her relief. "Oh, thank you, Waco." Impulsively she reached up and kissed his cheek. "See you later."

Miraculously, she had no trouble at all. It took all her concentration, and she had to go back and read the yellowed recipe again and again, but she came up with a perfectly passable chili, if she did say so herself. And there was a loaf of fresh sourdough bread in the pantry, lettuce for a green salad, sweet butter and Mexican beer. What else did she need?

Dessert. Visions of elegant mousses and three-layered chocolate cakes swam in her mind, and she reached for a cookbook again. She had only to glance at a few recipes to realize she was letting her success go to her head. There was no way she was going to fix that kind of dessert on such short notice. Better to dish out some ice cream from the freezer. She started to put the heavy book back on the shelf when something fell out of it to the floor.

She bent to pick it up. It was a photograph, and when she turned it faceup, what she saw stopped the breath in her throat.

The picture showed a younger Cal, without the mustache, and an achingly beautiful blonde who looked vaguely familiar. They were both laughing, heads thrown back, sunlight on their faces and wrapped in each other's arms. The inscription read, Cal and Janice on Their Honeymoon, with a date that was about eight years earlier.

"So what?" Marlo muttered, then repeated it and repeated it, trying hard to convince herself. This was an old relationship. It had to be. But why hadn't he told her he'd been married? She remembered asking him if he were married. He'd told her he wasn't. It would have been a logical time to bring up any past marriages. But he hadn't done that.

She put the picture into the pocket of her jeans and moved mechanically through the kitchen and out into the dining area, setting the places and the serving dishes. Any idiot could reason that Cal had loved other women before. This shouldn't be such a big shock to her, and she knew it. Yet for some illogical reason it was.

"That smells good," Cal said from the entryway, and she jerked around, managing a smile of welcome.

"I hope you like it," she said. "I'm not much of a cook, so this is an experiment."

He seemed to like it just fine, if asking for seconds was any sort of evidence. But he didn't say much. There was such a terrible constraint between them, as though the magic had been shattered. Could she pick up the pieces and get it back?

She glanced at his face as he buttered a bit of bread. His blue eyes were clouded and solemn. The usual spark of humor was gone. He was hurt, having second thoughts about their relationship, wondering why he'd gone to her apartment the night before. She could hear his doubts as though he'd spoken them aloud, and she wanted to yell at him, to tell him not to be such a fool and ruin everything. But she had her own doubts, and that stopped her. What would it take to clear them up? Perhaps a bit of courage.

She took a deep breath and plunged into the icy waters of uncertainty. "Cal, tell me about Janice."

It was as though she'd struck him with a blunt instrument. He stared at her, his eyes electric. "How do you know about Janice?" he asked, his controlled voice deadly with suppressed emotion.

She pulled the picture out of her pocket and handed it to him. He stared at it, his face unreadable, but the current of leashed anger was manifest. A spasm of pain flashed across his expression, and then he sent the picture spinning across the room. "Janice and I were married for a couple of years, that's all," he said casually. "How about some more of that beer?"

She ignored his evasive request. "You never told me you were married."

He shrugged as though the fact were negligible. "We were married, that's all. It was over in a couple of years. It's ancient history." He reached across her for the bottle, but she stopped him with a hand on his arm.

"It's not ancient history," she insisted, her voice trembling. "It's part of you."

His eyes were cold and white-hot at the same time. She could hardly bear to look into them. "It is not part of me," he said, his voice razor-sharp. "Not anymore."

Now that she'd come this far, she couldn't retreat. "Did you have any children?"

"No. No children." He jerked away from her grasp and got the bottle.

"Was that the only time you were married?"

"Yes." He poured the beer into his tall glass and took a long drink.

"Tell me what happened."

He stared at the wall as though he couldn't look at her. "It has absolutely nothing to do with us."

She felt as if she were being split in two. It would be easy to agree, to let it drop. But that wouldn't solve their problem. And something told her this was a step that had to be taken if there was to be any future for the two of them.

"If all you want," she began, her voice quavering, "is to sleep together for a couple of weeks and then say so long, you're right. It has nothing to do with us. But if you want more . . ."

He turned toward her, his eyes slightly wild. "Of course I want more," he told her harshly. "You know that."

She shook her head, forcing back tears. "How am I supposed to know that? You'll have to show me."

He stared at her fiercely, then cursed and turned his head away. "I met Janice through mutual friends," he began stonily. "She was an aspiring actress who'd come from the Midwest to try to make it in the movies. I fell in love with her right away. She was beautiful and exciting—like a firefly, always laughing and dancing and hard to catch hold of." His eyes clouded and he seemed to forget Marlo was there. "But I caught hold of her. And we got married." He took another sip of beer. "We were happy at first. I'd—it had been hard for me to commit myself, but I thought I'd done the right thing. Until I found out that Janice wanted to make it in Hollywood more than she wanted to make it with me."

He paused so long that Marlo had to speak. "What happened?" she asked quietly.

He looked up as though surprised to see her there. "What do you think happened?" he asked bitterly. "She had some crazy idea that because I knew a few people in show business I might be able to help her get parts. When that hope fell through, she turned to other sources. She started sleeping with producers. And it worked. You can see her on television practically any time you turn on the tube."

The face fell into place. "Janice Carter?"

He nodded. "Her stage name."

She had a moment of curiosity about what show business people Cal might know, but it was gone as soon as it came. She could feel the pain in him, and her heart was breaking. "You still love her, don't you?"

He seemed surprised. "No. Not at all." And strangely she believed him.

"But it still hurts . . ."

"Oh, yes." His laugh was cold as steel. "It hurts, all right." He grimaced. "She didn't want the divorce. She still calls me periodically, asking to try again."

"But you have no interest in that?"

"I'm not a very forgiving man, Marlo. I hold grudges. I've even been known to extract revenge when the offense called for it."

She shuddered, feeling suddenly cold. "You forgave me." She said it as a joke, something to lighten the mood.

"I didn't come back to forgive you, Marlo," he said, a flash of something devilish in his eyes. "I came back to make you pay. Didn't you know that?"

She loved him, and at that moment she was ready to pay any price. Slowly she turned her palms up before him. "Whatever I have," she whispered, "whatever you want, it's yours."

Cal gazed at her for a long time, and then the light of humor began to sparkle in his eyes. She wasn't sure just when the transformation began, but a time came when she was sure it had taken place, and she knew the magic was back.

"Do you really mean that?" he asked at last.

She nodded. "Yes, I really mean it."

"Well, I'm not sure I believe you," he said slowly, leaning back in his chair, his eyes narrowed arrogantly. "Convince me."

A tiny thrill raced down her spine and ended at the tip of her tailbone. "How can I do that?" she asked breathlessly, though she had an idea what he might have in mind.

A faint, cocky smile played about the corners of his wide mouth. "You'll find a way." Unfolding his long body, he rose and sauntered slowly to the couch, then flopped down against the pillows. "Think about it."

She stood nervously. Janice and horses and ad campaigns were all forgotten now. The promise implicit in his eyes was all she needed. She walked over to sit beside him on the couch, and then she lost her nerve.

"Oh, Cal," she cried, beseeching him, "I'm not sure what you—"

He put a finger to her lips to still her. His gaze was swirling with dark desire. "Don't talk," he murmured. "Just do it."

Her heart was pounding, and her fingers were trembling, but she was suddenly sure of what to do. Her hands flattened against the smooth fabric of his shirt, then slipped upward, feeling the heat of his body beneath. She reached for the top button and carefully pulled it free, then went to the next and did the same, until his shirt parted and she had access to his chest.

His heart thudded beneath her hands like a live animal. She scraped her fingertips across the rounded muscles, wove them into the thick, crisp pelt that covered him, reaching for the beat of his heart as though she would capture his essence by finding it.

"That's it," he muttered huskily. "You've got it."

She leaned over him, letting her ebony hair fall all around him, and pressed her face to his chest, taking in the rich, warm scent of his skin, the driving heat of his body, the excitement of his presence. Eyes closed, she began to explore the wide expanse with tiny kisses, letting her tongue flicker out to taste his slightly salty skin. He groaned and moved beneath her, but that only made her braver. Her kisses traveled down the valley of his rib cage, then stirred the hair that circled his navel, while her hands lightly stroked his sides. Her lips found the dark depression, and then her tongue entered it at the same time as her hand slipped beneath his belt, reaching slowly, slowly downward. Cal shuddered beneath her touch, reaching to pull her tighter, faster, harder.

And then suddenly their positions were reversed and Cal had control. She blinked up at him, almost groggily.

"If I'd known, lady, just how sweet and good you were going to be . . ."

She stretched against him, luxuriating in the feeling of loving companionship. "What's so special about me?" she whispered.

The laughter was in his voice again, and she loved to hear it. "There aren't many like you in the world," he drawled, teasing her. "You look so cool and polished on the surface. But that exterior only hides the molten lava that surges beneath." He was unbuttoning her shirt just as she'd unbuttoned his, and she was letting him.

"Molten lava?"

"Molten lava," he repeated, biting her earlobe. "Women who shouldn't be let out at night because they devour men as midnight snacks."

"Is that what I did?" she sighed lazily, arching as he pulled the shirt off. "Did I snack on you?"

"Absolutely," he breathed, running a hand across her flat stomach. "You left me a shell of my former self."

She giggled. "Poor Cal."

"Damned right. But that's what I get for messing with wild and wanton women." His thumb rubbed a path beneath her bra strap.

"Wantin' women?"

"That, too." He rose above her and gazed down at the picture she made in her lacy white bra. "You look so cute in this thing," he murmured, using his thumbs to stroke the nipples dark and erect beneath the fabric. "I almost hate to take it off." His snapped the bit of cloth away, his quick maneuver belying his words.

She gasped as he caressed her breasts. "I thought I was supposed to be doing this to you," she said breathlessly. "What happened?"

"You convinced me," he muttered, tugging at the button on her jeans. "Now I'm going to convince you."

She laughed softly, pulling his head to her as she arched to his touch. "Don't talk," she said, repeating what he'd told her. "Just do it."

He did, beginning with slow, sizzling ecstasy and building to an urgent frenzy that shattered the stillness and left them deliciously spent.

"I love you," she whispered, her face pressed into the hollow of his shoulder. But he didn't seem to hear her, and she didn't have the nerve to say it again.

Did he love her? She had no idea. He said he wanted more than a brief affair, but how much more? Cal James was a hard man. As he'd said, an unforgiving man. It would be dangerous to love him. And here she was, tumbling down the precipice.

"I'm sorry I didn't take better to horseback riding," she murmured, stroking her hand across his warm back.

He dug his fingers into her hair, tugging lightly. "Forget it. It was my fault. I don't know why it seemed so important for you to like it."

But she knew why, or anyway she hoped she did. "Give me another chance," she said, raising up to look into his face. "Let me try again."

He touched her cheek. "You're already sore. You want to be crippled?"

In truth, the thought of horseback riding made her wince. But she was ready to face anything that might bring him closer. "Give me another chance," she said stubbornly. "Tomorrow."

He searched her eyes. "No. I won't let you ride again tomorrow. But I have another idea. . . ."

HIS IDEA INVOLVED getting up very early in the morning. And when he roused her from a wonderful, warm dream in lyrical pastels to face the cold, gray, predawn hush, she had to wonder if horseback riding might not have been better after all.

"Come on," he said with disgusting heartiness as he sat on the edge of the bed they'd shared, pulling on his boots. "Rise and shine. Let's get out there."

She groaned and rolled over. "You have found more ways to torture me this weekend," she began, but he pulled off her covers and dragged her to her feet.

"You're a tough one to get up in the morning," he grumbled, reaching for her sweater. "How are you going to manage when you have a house full of kids to get off to school?"

She wondered if she'd heard right. "Kids?" she asked. "What kids?"

"Your kids." He made her raise her arms and pulled on the sweater. "I assume you expect to have some someday."

She wriggled into her jeans on her own. "I've never really thought about it." She peered at him suspiciously, fully awake by now. "Do you expect to have some someday?"

His face was guileless. "I've never really thought about it," he echoed. "Until lately..."

She started to reach for him, her heart pounding, but he'd already turned away.

"Let's get out there before the sun comes over the ridge," he said. "Everybody goes home at the first light, and we want to catch some of the action."

The subject of kids was obviously closed, and she wasn't at all sure what it had meant, anyway. If anything.

But what he had to show her out in the misty morning was wonderful. They hiked quickly to the hills. All around them lay sheets of mist covering the landscape with purple mystery. Looking more closely, Marlo could make out the heads of deer bobbing above the gossamer clouds, as though they were swimming in a swirling sea of foam. Little by little the sky got lighter and the mist evaporated until the whole wilderness world was spread out before them.

At first all she saw were the deer, the bucks with their antlers, the does playing tag with their half-grown young. But they walked farther, and she began to notice that rabbits jumped away at almost every step, long, rangy rabbits that reminded her more of Bugs Bunny than the furry little confections sold in pet shops.

"Jackrabbits," Cal said. "But down closer to the river you'll see cottontails, too."

There was a rustling of wings and a hawk flew by, circling higher and higher into a sky that was turning pearly as the sun nudged its way above the horizon.

"Over there," Cal whispered, pointing. "A pair of coyotes."

She watched them loping off, looking like underfed dogs. "I've never seen so many animals before outside of a zoo."

He put his arms around her from behind, holding her close against his body. "Do you like this?" he asked.

She sighed and leaned back into him. "I love it." *And you*, she added silently.

They returned to the house, and he cooked up a batch of pancakes, "since breakfast is my specialty," he told her. They shared the job of doing dishes, including those of the night before. And then they went out to look at some tamer animals.

"Cows are no problem," Cal said, introducing her to the cow pen. "They don't care a lot about humans, unless those humans get between them and the feeding trough. Then you might have trouble. Otherwise, they pretty much try to ignore our existence."

A large black-and-white member of the herd immediately put the lie to his words by coming up to the fence and licking Marlo right across the face with her huge, gummy tongue.

"Did you know you had this special attraction for animals?" Cal asked her, wiping away the evidence of the cow's affection with his handkerchief. "Or were you just keeping it a secret?"

"It's a total surprise to me." She chuckled. "Though I once knew a gerbil who seemed to like me a lot."

They bypassed the bull pen and went right to the stables. "I don't think I dare find out what they think of me," Marlo told Cal.

"I should give you time to get to know the horses. I think that's what went wrong yesterday," Cal said quite seriously. "We'll just hang around here for a while and take it slowly."

Marlo nodded, not caring what he made her do as long as he was there to do it with her. Cal took her up to meet each horse in turn, and she began to see that each animal had its own personality. Maybe someday—someday—she'd get up on a horse's back again. But not too soon.

She was beginning to enjoy it all when Waco called to them from the road. "If you can spare that little lady, I'd sure appreciate a hand with nursing that late calf," he said. "He needs a woman's touch."

Cal smiled down at her. "I think you can handle it," he said, even though she was shaking her head. "Go on with Waco. I'll finish up here."

She went, not sure what was in store, but after one look at the big-eyed calf, all her reservations went out the window. "His mother was accidentally killed," the old cowboy explained. "He's been okay at drinking from the bottle all week, but for some reason he's balking today."

Waco held the bottle, and she had the job of stroking the little animal and murmuring sweet nothings to calm him. His fur was short and soft, just beginning to turn coarse. It seemed a miracle to feel him gentle to her touch. His huge eyes rolled around to stare at her as he drank greedily from the bottle Waco held. Marlo found herself grinning with pride and exaltation, as though she'd performed the miracle on her own.

"See, what'd I tell you?" Waco crowed. "A woman's touch. That's all this baby needed." He laughed, holding up the empty bottle. "Yes, a woman's touch," he murmured again as they went outside the enclosure and leaned on the fence, watching the calf prance around. "We haven't had that around here since Cal's mother died."

"Cal was close to his mother, wasn't he?"

"Oh, yes, he adored her. But then we all did."

"And his father? What we he like?"

Waco shook his head. "Just like Cal. Cal thinks he hates his dad. He blames him for his mother being unhappy—for her death, even." He shrugged. "Someday he'll learn a little more charity, I hope. And then he'll see how much he and the old man are alike."

"How are they alike?"

Waco rubbed his forehead. "Both pigheaded. Stubbornest pair I've ever known. Both hard when they feel they have to be. And neither one will budge an inch in a fight." He looked sideways at her. "You want to be careful before you marry a man like that," he cautioned. "Cal's mother was miserable, but she was a fragile flower that should've been kept better. You're sturdier, I'd say."

Marlo wondered if he'd have made that judgment if he'd seen her on the horse the day before. She was just about to ask how Janice had stacked up in the sturdy department when Cal appeared, and the question died on her lips.

"You trying to steal my girl from me, Waco?" he teased, coming up and putting his arms around her shoulders.

"Nope." Waco grinned. "My girl-stealin' days are over." He gave Cal a slap on the back as he passed. "But I'd say this one's worth stealin', so you better make sure you get her secured pretty fast, boy." He gave Marlo an exaggerated wink. "It'd be nice to have her around," he commented just before he disappeared around the corner of the building.

"Waco approves," Cal said. "What more could I ask for?"

But he was only kidding. Marlo knew that. If only she also knew what he had in mind for them.

11

THE DAY OF THE PRESENTATION had arrived. The red-letter day. Marlo wasn't scared, exactly.

"A better word would be numb," she told Jeri as they prepared to present their campaign.

But she knew everything she wanted to say. The comprehensives were gorgeous. She couldn't have been more organized or better prepared. If only her whole career weren't riding on this, she would probably be quietly confident.

"I wish you'd come in with me," she'd told Cal that morning as they lay in bed, bodies entwined. "I could bring you on at the last moment—my clincher."

"No way," he'd said flatly. "I signed on to do the pictures, not to pitch your case."

She'd sighed and struck a noble pose. "Then I guess I'll just have to do it all by myself," she'd said grandly before he'd ruined her act with a well-placed tickle.

They'd had a wonderful time all week. They'd come back from the ranch and settled into her apartment as though they'd always lived together. She'd worked hard to get the presentation ready on time, but there'd been opportunities for play, too.

When she refused to go to Disneyland in the daytime with him, he took her at night, and they danced to the Dixieland bands and rode Big Thunder Mountain in the moonlight. The next night he took her to Hollywood to see the stars embedded in the sidewalks.

But mostly they'd been together, alone and satisfied with the company. Marlo loved Cal and that love grew as she got to know him better. It changed her whole outlook on life, made her think about bridal veils and diapers and things she'd never dreamed would become important to her. The only trouble was that she had no idea how he felt.

She'd been brave before in confronting him with difficult questions, but a part of her had wanted to hold off on this one until after the presentation. And she'd listened to that little voice. She wanted to be able to concentrate and do it right. And she didn't want to ruin what they had by pushing him. So she put off the questions and lived for the moment—the many soaring, delicious moments they had together.

But today was the presentation, and she had to forget all about him. She marched into the boardroom with Jeri at her side and a confident smile on her face, but inside she was tight with anxiety. This had to work. If it didn't, she was finished at Grayson's and perhaps in the industry as a whole. So it had to work. But what if it didn't? What if she went blank right in front of everyone? What if . . . ? She silently ordered the inner voices to be still and looked around at the people she was going to be facing.

Art Grayson sat at the head of the table. Mr. Caron was at his side. But Mr. Caron had brought along two vice presidents and the brand manager, Joe Taggert. That made four against three, and Marlo knew that numbers mattered in these sessions. She wished she'd insisted that Cal come, too.

Mr. Caron nodded in greeting and turned to talk to Art. Marlo and Jeri began to set up their visual support the way they'd rehearsed. As they were finishing, Joe Taggert sidled up alongside Marlo with an oily smirk. "How's your microwave?" he asked.

She stared at him blankly. "My what?"

"Your microwave. Did it cause a lot of damage?"

The memory of their night out the week before flooded back. "Oh. Oh, that. No, not really." A little devilry spiked the rest of her reply. "We had to evacuate the kitchen, of course."

His mouth formed a little circle. "Did you?"

"Oh, yes. Well, just to be safe. All those little microwaves everywhere, you know."

"Yes, yes." He nodded vigorously. "I had heard they did that. You never know."

"No, you never do." Marlo hated herself for teasing him, yet decided it served him right for trying to put the make on her. Besides, how any man who knew so little about modern appliances could be brand manager in an electronics firm was beyond her.

He backed away as though afraid "those little microwaves" might still be contaminating Marlo to some degree, and she focused on the coming struggle. She and Jeri had just settled into their chairs around the gigantic, highly polished table when the door to the room opened again and in walked Ted and Jill, each with a triumphant smile for Marlo and a portfolio. They sat down on the other side of the table, and Marlo leaned toward Mr. Grayson.

"Why are they here?" she asked. The Caron people were talking among themselves, and she felt confident they wouldn't notice her unease.

Her boss knew who she meant. He glanced at his two copywriters, nodded briefly and turned back to Marlo. "Ted's got a proposal of his own, Marlo, just in case yours doesn't pan out."

Inside, Marlo went white-hot. She was furious, and now she would have to spend valuable time and energy to make sure it didn't show. So he had no faith in her at all! And Ted had more power than she'd realized. There was no point in being angry, she knew. These were givens that she now had to deal with. She smiled at Mr. Caron and decided to take the bull by the horns.

"If Mr. Caron is ready, Mr. Grayson, I'll begin."

On the whole things went well. Jeri set up the easel and it didn't fall. The air conditioner didn't go on the blink. Marlo didn't trip and land on her face once during the entire hour. And no one fell asleep.

"The picture will fill two-thirds of the page," she explained as she passed around the photographs. "As you can see, the headline will read A Noble Tradition in bold type, and the copy will be concerned with the taming of the West and individualism, developing logically into the use of the wrist radio. Caron's wrist radio."

She was eloquent, she was dynamic, she was persuasion itself. And the pictures were fabulous. The two vice presidents loved the campaign. So did the brand manager. Only Mr. Caron was skeptical. Too bad he was the one who mattered.

"I just don't know," he kept saying, squinting at the charts. "Westerns to sell wrist radios?"

"But that's not the point," Marlo tried to explain as gently as possible. "It's not Westerns per se. It's the idea of strength and integrity that we're trying to convey. It's a hearkening back to a time of firmer values."

Mr. Caron shook his head. "Can they really receive radio signals that far out in the wilderness?"

Out of the corner of her eye, Marlo could see Ted gearing up. She looked quickly at Mr. Grayson, ready to insist on more time before Ted got his chance, but he was concentrating on the photographs she'd passed around and not paying any attention to the signals she was sending.

"Who's the model?" he asked suddenly, not looking up from the picture.

Marlo blinked. "His name is Cal James," she responded.

His brow furrowed. "The first name starts with an R," he said reflectively.

"I—I don't think so. His full name is California..." she began, but Art's face lit up.

He yelled, "Robert California Carillo James! That's it."

Marlo had no idea what her boss was driving at, or why he cared. "It could be, I suppose—"

"You suppose!" Mr. Grayson was laughing. "You suppose!" He turned to the Caron people and gestured for them to come back to the table. "Sit down, gentlemen, we've got a whole new angle here."

Marlo was bewildered. She glanced at Ted suspiciously, but when she realized he looked more worried than she felt, she relaxed. If Ted hated this, it couldn't be all bad.

"Robert California Carillo James," he repeated to Mr. Caron. "That name ring a bell for you?"

Mr. Caron frowned. "You can't mean Windsor James's kid, can you? Working as a model? Let me see that."

Art pushed the photographs in front of the older man, and Mr. Caron examined them. "Are you sure that's who this is?"

Art nodded. "It's him, all right."

Mr. Caron shook his head. "I don't know. I wouldn't have recognized him. I remember seeing pictures of him as a boy, but that was years ago. That sensational divorce case . . ."

"Windsor James's only son," Art Grayson said happily. "Windsor went to school with my father. I've been to his house in New York. I recognized his kid right away."

"Mr. Grayson," Marlo broke in at last. "Who is Windsor James?"

"Last year *Fortune* named him one of the ten wealthiest self-made men in the world, that's all. And he's the Caron Man's father." He chortled. "What luck!"

Cal's father one of the richest men in the world? Marlo wanted to tell Art to quit kidding around. If they knew Cal, they'd know . . . what? Just what did she know, after all? One of the richest men in the world. A terrible emptiness was growing in the pit of her stomach. She felt as if he were fading away from her.

Mr. Caron seemed intrigued, but he was a cautious man, and that caution was still evident. "How can we make sure people know who he is?"

Grayson shrugged. "That's easy. We trumpet it! I've seen him mentioned in Where Are They Now? features. No one seems to know he's still around." He pointed down the table. "We'll put Ted on it. He's got contacts at *People* and at the *Today Show*. Before the month is out, everyone in the country will know who your Caron Man is, and everyone will be talking about him."

"And the wrist radios," Mr. Caron reminded him, beginning to get excited.

"Of course."

"I can make some calls this evening," Ted put in. He hadn't moved from his seat, but Marlo had the distinct impression of having just received an elbow in the ribs. "In fact, I'm having cocktails with the editor of the *Weekly Wire*. We can start dropping hints by the time Sunday's paper hits the streets."

Marlo sat down. She felt light-headed and slightly sick. On one hand, there was this news about Cal that she hadn't been able to fully assimilate yet. On the other, there was Ted waiting around every corner to pounce on any advantage. She'd let her guard down, and he'd sensed her weakness. If she didn't watch out, he'd win whether she got the account or not.

"I think we'll have to get Cal's okay," she said shakily.

"What for?" Mr. Grayson thundered. "He's signed a contract, hasn't he?"

"Yes, but—"

"Then he's our boy for the duration. Whether he likes it or not."

That sick feeling was getting stronger. Suddenly she knew beyond a shadow of a doubt that Cal wasn't going to like it at all. Everyone was talking at once. Even Jill was involved. Only Marlo sat apart, and she felt the rising excitement of the others like a tidal wave washing over her.

She wished they would all be quiet so she could think. Her head was beginning to pound, and her eyes felt hot and sandy.

Mr. Caron was really enthusiastic now, pounding the table and laughing. She should be happy. She knew her campaign was going to give him the market share he wanted. The only stumbling block had been his reluctance to go out on a limb and try it. Now that reluctance had been overcome. That was the important thing. After all, she'd been working toward this moment all her life.

So why couldn't she feel happy about it? Why did she feel this deep, awful dread?

The feeling only got worse as she drove home. Her headache was so bad she could hardly see straight. She didn't let herself try to think things through. Cal was waiting. He would explain everything.

She found him coming out of the shower, a towel wrapped around his waist. He looked so fresh and clean that suddenly she wished she could forget all that had happened and just run to him, hold him, love him. But that was impossible.

"Hi there," he said, his lopsided smile bright with welcome. "How'd it go?"

She stood in the doorway, one hand on the wall. "Is your name really Robert California Carillo James?" she asked breathlessly, and the air seemed to quiver between them as she waited for the answer.

The smile left Cal's face. The hard, wary look she'd seen so often at first was back. "No. Not anymore."

But she saw yes in his face. "Is your father very, very rich?"

He shrugged. "Probably. I don't keep track."

She put one hand over her mouth, as if to stop a scream. Somehow this was hitting her much harder than she'd imagined. He really was this strange alien being Art Grayson had described. Her Cal wasn't her Cal. He was someone totally different. "Why didn't you tell me?" she managed to grate out.

"Tell you? Tell you what? That the man I used to call my father was rich? Who cares? I don't see him anymore. And he doesn't see me."

"Are you rich?" she asked bluntly.

He hesitated. "I'm doing okay," he allowed grudgingly. "You knew I had the ranches."

"Yes, but . . ." Not rich. There was something so inhibiting about his being rich. "I suppose you'll inherit . . ."

"I wouldn't take anything from him," Cal said harshly. "I don't need it."

She walked very slowly and carefully into the room and put her purse down on the table. "I wish you'd told me that you're famous," she said.

"I'm not famous. My father is."

"Yes, but . . ." She turned back to look at him. "The presentation went fine except that Mr. Caron wasn't convinced. He needed one final shove over the edge to commit himself."

Cal's face was hard and impassive. "And?"

She looked down at her hands, wondering why her fingers had gripped one another so tightly. "He was wavering and about to turn me down. And Ted was sitting there with his tongue hanging out, waiting for his chance. And then—and then Mr. Grayson recognized your picture. He knows your father." She stopped, wetting her very dry lips.

"And?" His voice was hard as steel on steel.

"So he brought up your identity and how that would go over with the public and how you could—could help by doing interviews—"

"Marlo!"

"And Mr. Caron thought it was wonderful and went for the whole package," she burst out quickly before he could stop her. "So I've won, if you'll just go along with—"

He was at her side and taking her hands in his own firm grip. "I can't do that, Marlo," he said evenly. "You know that, don't you? I can't do it, and I wouldn't, even if I could."

Her headache was so intense that it sent spasms of pain down her shoulders. "But, Cal," she said weakly, "Ted will win. You know how he is. One false step and he'll push his way in. I'll lose the account. I'll lose my job. I'll lose everything."

His blue eyes narrowed, then he dropped her hands. "Everything?" he repeated bitterly.

Marlo turned and went into the kitchen, rummaging through a cabinet for aspirin. She couldn't think. She only knew that her world seemed to be falling apart around her. Cal followed her and waited while she took the pills, then caught her by the shoulders.

"You know, winning isn't all there is, Marlo," he told her earnestly. "Those things aren't really important in the long run."

What was he giving her, a lecture? She closed her eyes. She didn't want to hear it. "They are to me," she replied.

His fingers tightened on her shoulders. "Why?"

She pulled away and walked toward the living room. This was no time to explain to him about her father, about how she'd worked so hard for his approval all these years. Didn't he understand? No, of course not. He didn't care what his own father thought of him. He'd cast him off and wanted nothing more to do with him. How could he understand?

Someday she'd try to make him see it. But not now. Not here. "I have to prove that I can do it," she said, thinking of all the people at Grayson's who'd scorned her and talked behind her back. "That's all." She sank down onto the couch and he sat beside her. "I have to win."

She closed her eyes and put her head back, expecting him to take her in his arms. She needed his comfort desperately. Surely he could sense that. But he didn't seem to. He sat very still for a long time, and finally he spoke without touching her.

"I never thought I'd be recognized. When you told me my name wouldn't be used, I thought I was okay on that score. If I'd foreseen this happening, I would have saved us both a lot of trouble."

Trouble. She formed the word with her lips, but didn't say it aloud. Was that all she was to him now? Trouble? She wanted to reach for him, but she couldn't.

His voice went on, low and far away. "When my father married my mother, she was a free spirit. She'd grown up wild on the ranch, and she loved the wind in her hair. He took her to New York and made her part of his ambition machine. She was supposed to hostess parties and cozy up to important people for him— things she just wasn't equipped to do. And when he realized she wasn't going to be an asset, he cast her off like so much extra baggage. He crushed the life out of her. I'll never forgive him for that."

She could hear the depth of emotion in his voice. He'd never talked about this to anyone before. Instinctively she knew it.

"He worked hard at it. I'll give him that. And he succeeded beyond his wildest dreams by being in the right place at the right time, and by stepping on anyone who got in his way. He wanted me to go in with him when I graduated from college. He couldn't understand why I chose the ranch instead. That's something he'll never forgive me for."

She frowned, sensing he was telling her all this for a reason. What was it? What could the connection possibly be?

"My father's ambition was the most destructive force in my family," he said evenly. "Users are not my favorite people."

Did he think she wanted to use him the way his father had used his fragile mother? This wasn't the same thing at all. But he felt strongly about it; she could see that. She felt for him and for what had happened to his mother. Thinking hard, she tried to come up with an idea to make it easier for him.

"You know," she said tentatively, "I could possibly talk Mr. Grayson out of the television guest appearances. If you'd just do the print interviews . . ."

The fire was back in his eyes. "You don't get it, do you?" he said in a voice as cold as a prairie blizzard. "I'm not doing the ad campaign now. Not under any conditions."

She stared back at him. It hadn't really sunk in yet that he meant every word he'd just said. "You've got a contract."

He shrugged arrogantly, his head high. "Tell Grayson to sue me."

She sat up higher. Her head was still pounding, and she was very confused. "But—but, Cal, why do you say that? Surely you can handle a couple of columnists asking a few simple questions. What's the harm?"

There was a storm gathering in his eyes. The warm, loving Cal who'd cuddled with her all week was gone. In his place was a cold, wild-eyed stranger. There seemed to be no way she could reach him, and she sat staring at him, feeling at a loss.

He rose from the couch, hitching the towel higher on his hips. "I knew this was a mistake from the beginning. I'm getting out of here."

"Out of here?" Her breath stopped in her throat. He couldn't leave. Not now. But she couldn't breathe, couldn't move to stop him.

"Excessive ambition has always turned me off," he said coldly. "You've got it. I don't need it."

She swung around, aghast. "What are you talking about?" She reached for him, but he evaded her touch. "What's so terrible about ambition?" she asked. She was hurt and feeling a bit defensive. "I suppose you have no ambition? You run those two big ranches, and you don't care how well you do at it? I can't quite believe that, Cal."

"Sure I care how I do at it. I try to make them both the best they can be." He turned toward the bedroom again. "But I don't use other people to do it."

Use other people. That was what he thought she did. The horror of his accusation wrapped around her, and she couldn't think of a thing to say in response. "Don't go," she managed to grate out. "If you go, you won't come back."

"You're right there," he growled in return. "I have no intention of coming back."

She sat numbly while he dressed and packed. She was hot and cold and fearful and angry by turn. If he left, she would lose. That sentence kept repeating itself over and over in her head. If he left, she would lose.

There was much more that would slip through her fingers, things impossible to itemize. And because losing them would be so painful, she couldn't allow herself to think about them. Instead, she kept the obvious in the forefront. If he left, she would lose. That was something she could deal with. The other cut too deeply to stand.

He walked through the living room on his way out. She stared down at her hands, unwilling to face him.

"Marlo," he said, and his voice had lost its anger, "I don't want to leave you like this."

She looked up quickly, hope shining in her eyes, but he put out a hand as though to hold it back, and she noticed that his eyes were still diamond hard.

"I once had to make a choice," he said softly, "between my father's love and the sort of life I could lead and keep my integrity intact. I made that choice." He stopped, his gaze searching hers. "Now I'm asking you to make a similar choice. Give it all up and come with me." He let that sink in for a moment, then added, "Or we're through."

Hope died painfully. Give it all up? All she'd worked for all her life? She looked away. "That's ridiculous," she whispered. "You can't ask me to make a choice like that."

He watched her for a moment, then went on. "Remember the old saying about how it's not whether you win or lose, but how you play the game that counts?"

"Of course, but that's Utopian," she answered without looking at him.

"I guess that's what I am, then. I want to live a Utopian life away from all the winners and losers. Sorry you don't share my values." He turned toward the doorway, and then he was gone. And she hadn't really done a thing to try to stop him.

12

ART GRAYSON TOOK the Caron account away from Marlo and gave it to Ted. She'd known he would, and when the time came, she hardly even felt the pain. She was able to stand in front of his desk with her head held high.

"I'm sorry I didn't come through for you, Mr. Grayson," she said, and for once he didn't urge her to use his first name.

He watched her for a long moment, his face twisted with indecision. She had the distinct impression he'd planned to fire her, but in the end he couldn't bring himself to do it.

"Listen," he said gruffly. "There's this little account that's been batted around from one creative team to another. No one seems to know how to get a handle on it. If you want to try..."

She smiled wanly, grateful for another chance, but wary of getting excited one more time. "I'll do my best," she told him, knowing how hollow that seemed after all that had happened. "What—what are you planning to do about Cal James breaking his contract?" she couldn't help asking.

"Not a thing. We're not doing that ad series anymore. There's no use pursuing it."

She didn't know if she was relieved or sorry. Even a lawsuit would be better than no contact with him at all. But her ideas for the Caron campaign were now a thing of the past. Ted's presentation had been hurriedly assembled, and Mr. Caron had loved it. The fact that it was based on the same old trends only made him feel safe. Marlo knew he wasn't going to broaden his market base with Ted's campaign, but it was out of her hands.

She picked up the information on her new account and took it back to the office. "Come on in here," she told Jeri. "We're still in business. Let's take a look at this." She noticed a strange look on Jeri's face. "What's the matter?"

"Well, it's like this, boss." Jeri tried to smile. "I've been transferred."

"Oh. Oh, of course." There was a lump in her throat, but she managed to talk around it. "That's okay. This account is so small I won't need you." She blinked back tears. Funny. She hadn't cried over Cal. Why was she getting so emotional over Jeri leaving? "Who gets you now?"

Jeri looked down at her desk and turned a little red. "Ted," she said in a voice that was barely audible.

Marlo whirled and stared at the wall, blinking very quickly. "Maybe I should offer to move out, and he could move right in," she said bitterly. "That would be less hassle for everyone concerned." Her voice sounded strained and ugly. "Well, I guess Ted's got what he always wanted, hasn't he?"

Jeri moved toward her. "It's not really his fault, you know," she began, and Marlo spun to glare at her.

"Not Ted's fault! Maybe not, but it's not as if he hasn't been trying to make it his fault." She backed away from Jeri's hand. There was only one other time in her life that she'd felt more deserted than she felt now. "Why don't you just go ahead and clean out your desk?" she said quickly, keeping a grip on her emotions. "I've got work to do."

It would be easy to let herself get paranoid, she realized. The world did seem to be against her right now. But she did have the little account Grayson had given her, and she immersed herself in work on that right away, keeping the demons at bay.

The account was for a small Los Angeles company called Bibi's Olives. They'd developed spicier varieties of olives that had made quite a local reputation. They now wanted to market them statewide, and Marlo's job was to work up a print campaign.

"Olives," she sighed as she looked over the halfhearted attempts others in the agency had made on the account. "No wonder this has been a football."

She met with the Bibi people and she liked them. There were no vice presidents or brand managers for the olive company. There was only Bibi and the fourteen relatives who worked for him. And the olives were surprisingly delicious. Marlo was determined to do her best for them.

She got Angel Cortez to work with her, and together they spent hours throwing ideas back and forth. Angel turned out to be quite a cartoonist, and Marlo got him to work up some sketches of olives with faces—some with glasses and others with bow ties or punk hairdos.

"Cute," she told him, nodding her head. "We're going to do something with this."

"Good," Angel sighed with a stretch and a yawn. "Wake me up when you decide what that something is."

"Oh, sorry." It was almost nine o'clock again. "You go on home. I'll play with this for a while longer and let you know what I come up with in the morning."

She worked late every night. As long as she was working, she didn't have to think. Though she did get a pang every time she passed Jeri's empty desk, for the most part she was able to hold off the bad memories while she was involved with the account. It was when she went home to her lonely bed that she would begin to shake.

She missed him. Oh, how she missed him! When she let herself think about it, a wrenching ache seemed to split her in two. In a few short days he'd changed her life, and she would never be the same again.

She'd tried to think over what had happened to their love affair, but everything was still too jumbled to really pick apart. He'd gotten so angry when she asked him to do the interviews, as though he thought she was using him. She could understand that now. At the time she'd been shocked and defensive at his attitude. But she'd had time to think, and now she could understand. She no longer blamed him for bowing out on the ads.

But what she couldn't understand or forgive was the way he'd left. How could he turn his back on her the way he did? The answer was so simple: he didn't love her. There could be no other explanation.

He hadn't tried to contact her in any way. She assumed he'd gone back to his ranch. She knew she could pick up a telephone and call him, and there were times when she got as far as putting her hand on the phone.

But she couldn't go through with it. If he didn't love her, she wasn't going to beg him to come back. She'd done enough begging in her life and look where it had gotten her.

Still, life seemed so empty now. There was no one to share a joke with, no one to hold her at night. The loneliness had been bearable before because it was all she was used to. But now she knew what else life could hold. The days stretched long and hollow without him, and the nights, filled with ghosts and whispers of what they'd had together, were almost impossible to get through without tears.

Why didn't he call or write, or send some sort of message? Could he really put what they'd had together behind him so easily? Did he ever stop in the middle of his day and think of her? She could close her eyes and smell him, feel him, love him again. Sometimes she thought she might go crazy loving him.

She saw Ted now and then in the halls. Mostly she was able to elude him, but one afternoon they got caught on the same elevator.

"What?" He pretended to be surprised. "You still here? I thought you'd be long gone."

"Hanging on by the skin of my teeth," she said as cheerfully as possible.

He stood staring at her even after the doors had opened on his floor. She was sure for just a moment that he wanted to wish her luck, or tell her it hadn't been personal—something like that. But he didn't quite know how to do it. And finally he gave up.

"Then I hope you have a good dentist," he said instead, reverting to his usual wit. "You're going to need one."

She just smiled at him, and he seemed confused. *Don't end up like Ted,* she told herself as she watched him walk away. Don't let fighting become the only way you know how to communicate.

She was enjoying working with Angel more and more. His quiet confidence and sometimes raucous sense of humor seemed to steady her, and she found herself spending more and more time down in the art department and less time in her office.

"How's this?" she said late one afternoon, thrusting her pad in front of him. She'd used cutouts of some of his cartoon olives to illustrate her idea.

The headline read Remember the Good Old Days When Olives Knew Their Place? Under the headline was a picture of a quiet bowl of normal olives, very drab and dull. Then came the second headline. You've Come a Long Way, Bibi! it shrieked, and beneath it was a riotous scene of cartoon olives hamming it up. "Bibi's Olives," said the copy text, "are a new experience in taste."

"Great." Angel grinned. "How about a series of different ads, each showing Bibi's Olives somewhere you wouldn't expect olives to show up, like an elegantly dressed olive at the opera—"

"Or a rowdy bunch of olives at a baseball game—"

"A political rally—"

"In bikinis at the beach—"

"In curlers having a slumber party—"

"With a tag line," she suggested. "How's this? 'If it ain't Bibi's, it's the pits'?"

The ideas flew, and they laughed until they were sore. "Let's go tell the Bibis," Marlo suggested on the spur of the moment.

Angel glanced at his watch. "It's almost six o'clock."

"Who cares? I want to tell them about it."

Angel raised an eyebrow. "No formal presentation with Mr. Grayson and the Bibis lined up in a row?"

She laughed and began to gather their materials. "None of that. Just people, face-to-face. That's the way I like it."

"You know," Angel said speculatively, "you ought to get out of here. Soon."

She glanced at him curiously. "What are you talking about?"

"You don't belong here."

She stopped and frowned, ready to be insulted. "Why not?"

"You like to work with people, but you like to do copy, too. In fact, you want to do it all, from the first contact with the client to the final proofs on the copy. That's not the way things operate in a big agency like this. You ought to open up your own little place."

What a crazy idea. "Are you kidding?"

"No," he said seriously, "I'm not. Oh, I don't mean here in Los Angeles. It's overrun by giants. I mean in some little town somewhere, where you can be the big cheese and run it all by yourself."

She smiled at him, slightly bemused. "I've never lived in a small town."

He shrugged. "It's just like a city, only smaller."

"I'd need an artist," she joked. "Would you come work for me?"

"In the right little town I just might."

She dismissed the whole thing with a wave of her hand. "Come on. Let's see what the Bibis think of this."

The Bibis loved it. They loved it so much they insisted on taking Marlo and Angel out for pizza to celebrate. All the cousins and nieces and nephews came along, from the ninety-year-old patriarch of the clan to the six-month-old baby of Antonio Bibi himself, and they had a wonderful, if somewhat noisy, time. But all the fun only made her apartment seem that much emptier when she got home.

Weekends were the worst. Peter and Mary Jane tried hard to get her out into the action, but she played matchmaker, putting the two of them together and taking care of two birds with one stone. It was miserable to be alone and to remember, but it was more miserable to be out with people she didn't really want to be out with, pretending to have a good time. Once her two neighbors found each other, she hardly saw a sign of either of them again.

Meanwhile, her ads for the Bibis seemed to be going over well. Mr. Grayson even invited her to lunch with some other account executives. Jill was invited along, too, and spent the entire time glued to Marlo's side as though they'd been fast friends for years.

At one point Marlo got up to visit the powder room, and Jill decided to come along. As they wound their way through the crowded restaurant, Marlo spotted a couple in a secluded booth, and the sight stopped her in her tracks. It was Ted and Jeri, their heads close together, oblivious to the world around them. A business lunch this was not.

"I can't believe it," Marlo blurted out before she thought.

Jill snickered at her side. "You've got to hand it to Jeri," she said. "She's had the hots for Ted for years. It looks like she finally got him, doesn't it?"

Marlo hurried on to the powder room. "But she couldn't stand him," she murmured, feeling as though her feet had been knocked out from under her again.

"Are you kidding? Everyone knew she was crazy about him. He even used to make jokes about it."

Everyone but me, Marlo thought. How many times had she told Jeri things that Ted could have used against her? How much of what Ted did get wind of had come from Jeri? It made her sick to be that suspicious, but what else could she think?

When they got back from lunch, she went down to the art department and told Angel what had happened. "What do you think? Am I being paranoid again?"

Angel shrugged, a smile just barely curving his lips. "Probably not. People will do a lot of things when they're in love. That's why love is considered a form of insanity."

She sighed in exasperation. "It is not, and you know it."

"Didn't you?" he asked quietly.

She stared at him. "Didn't I what?"

"Do a lot of crazy things when Cal was here?"

She blinked at him. "Yes," she whispered, and her heart twisted painfully in her chest. And she'd let him go. That was the craziest of all.

Angel nodded. "So Jeri did some things, too. Forgive her. You two were good friends once. You should be again."

"I'm not a very forgiving man." Cal's voice echoed through her head. He'd certainly proved that to be true. He hadn't shown any sign of forgiving her for what he seemed to think she'd done. He still must think she wanted to use him, that she hardly cared for anything but her own ambition. He might never forgive that. But had she forgiven him?

She walked over to the corner and picked up Angel's guitar, running her hand over the smooth wood. She could close her eyes and remember Cal strumming the chords and singing that silly Western song to her. The sound seemed to come softly from the shadows, as though the notes had collected there, waiting for her to recall them. ". . . crazy for her laughter, I burn to taste her smile . . ."

Her breath caught in her throat. Yes, she would forgive him. She would do almost anything to get him back. Almost anything. If she only knew what would work!

Angel seemed to be reading her mind. "I knew who he was the first time he walked in here, you know," he said calmly, putting his pencils in neat rows across his drawing board.

She swung around, then put down the guitar. "Why didn't you tell me?"

"It wasn't any of my business. Besides, I didn't know you weren't aware of it."

She came over and leaned on her elbows, staring at him. "How did you know?"

He smiled his secretive smile, avoiding her eyes. "I like to keep up with the comings and goings of people who are related to the early California families. His mother's people on her father's side were Carillos."

"And?"

"I keep scrapbooks on everything I read in the papers or in magazines because someday I'm going to do a book on them."

"The Carillos?"

"All the descendants of the Californios. Including your Cal James."

She winced at his words. "He's not mine," she said stonily. "I haven't seen him since the day he refused to go ahead with the Caron ads. I don't think I'll ever see him again."

She rose and began to pace across the studio.

Angel leaned back in his chair, watching her. "I get the feeling that you blame him for losing the account. That you hold it against him for not wanting to do the shoot."

"I never said that."

"I know you didn't. But I've got eyes." He watched her pace for another moment, then went on. "Did it ever occur to you that he wouldn't do the pictures because he didn't want to hurt his father?"

She looked at him, then turned away. "He hates his father."

Angel shook his head. "Do any of us really hate our father?"

Marlo stopped, stunned. He was right, of course. Look at all her father had done to her. Or hadn't done, rather. Angry and resentful as she'd often been, she'd never been able to say she hated him. Loving too much was more like it.

Angel started talking again. "Maybe he decided he couldn't market his father's name that way. Or maybe he felt it would be too much like rubbing his father's nose in it, to make it so public that he'd chosen the ranch over his father's business. Who knows?" He got up and began to shrug into his jacket. "Anyway, I just think you ought to take that into consideration before you write the guy off."

She watched numbly as he left the room. Write Cal off—she would never be able to do that. But she had done things he'd considered unforgivable. Would her unforgiving man listen to an apology? It made her shiver to think of it.

She invited Jeri over for dinner the next night. Jeri was surprised, but she came. After a fairly stiff beginning they cleared the air between them, and by the time they'd polished off a bottle of wine, they were joking together as they'd done in the past.

"Yes, I've loved Ted for years," Jeri admitted when Marlo brought it up. "But he always made fun of me. And I was so angry. But now—" she colored and looked prettier than Marlo had ever seen her "—we seem to be getting closer...."

Marlo didn't ask how much Jeri might have told Ted about her own business. It didn't seem the time or the place. And, strangely, she didn't really care much anymore.

Angel had been right about Jeri, and she began to think he might be right about Cal as well. Certainly there had to be more to Cal's refusal to do the ads than pure stubbornness, as she'd thought at first. He'd agreed to do the ads just to help her. He'd disliked the work from the beginning, and he certainly hadn't needed the money. She should have been more grateful. And when his identity was discovered and he'd refused to let his father's fame be used to sell wrist radios, she hadn't even tried to understand his position. Slowly she was beginning to see that she may have been the one who'd been stubborn.

WEEKS WENT BY and public reaction to the Bibi ads began to build. Art Grayson called her into his office and greeted her at the door enthusiastically.

"I've just had a call from Antonio Bibi," he said. "He's talking about going national in six months. Retailers from all over the state, and some from as far away as Alaska, are calling in, begging for shipments." He pretended to give her a playful punch in the shoulder. "You've got yourself a hit here, Marlo."

She smiled. It felt good to have the pieces fall into place again. Good, but not nearly as good as she'd expected.

"I want you to draw up plans for the national campaign," he told her. "Oh, and while you're at it, there's another little company, a toy maker, that's having trouble getting the right approach. See what you can do with it."

No one said it in so many words, but it looked as if she was back in business. She felt a sense of quiet satisfaction, but not a lot of joy. Somehow the joy seemed to have gone out of her life, as a song whose tune she couldn't quite remember.

She knew what it was. Cal was gone. But she had her work, she kept reminding herself. That should be enough. And it would be, if she could only forget . . .

The weekend at Lake Arrowhead came and went. She wasn't invited, but she hardly noticed. Summer began to fade into fall. Days followed one another in a chain of feverish activity. The Bibi campaign for national exposure was going well, and Antonio Bibi was talking grandly of television commercials. The toy maker liked what Marlo had come up with so far, but hadn't decided on a full series of ads yet. And the Caron ads were falling on their collective face.

Marlo had avoided any gossip about what Ted was doing, but when Mr. Grayson called her in to a meeting and she found half the agency staff there, including Ted, she knew something was up. She sat by Angel and waited to hear what it was.

Grayson didn't spare time or feelings. "The Caron people are livid," he announced to one and all. "Sales have actually gone down since Ted's campaign was introduced."

Marlo glanced at her competitor and felt a swift flash of admiration. His failure was the reason behind this entire meeting, and yet he was managing to sit there and look like a British colonel sipping a gin and tonic on a veranda. The man had guts.

"They're junking the entire thing," Art went on. "And Mr. Caron was on the horn to me just now asking about what happened to that pretty lady and her idea for a Western extravaganza."

Marlo looked up, mouth open, and Grayson stared at her. "Yes, you," he said. Then he turned back to the rest of them. "I want you all to look at these."

He pulled a stack of blowups from the table in front of him and began distributing them around the room. Marlo knew what they must be, but avoided looking at them until three arrived in a pile in front of her.

The top one was Cal on a horse, looking just as he had at the ranch. He was gazing off at the horizon as though expecting adventure to be waiting. Marlo felt a lump begin to grow in her throat, and she quickly passed the picture on.

"I want you to look long and hard at these," Art was saying. "I want feedback from everybody. Tell me what you think, no matter what. I want truth."

Marlo glanced down at the next picture. Cal was leaning forward in the saddle, his hat turned down as though against a fierce wind. She passed that picture on, too.

"In my view this is creative work at its best," Art went on. "Marlo Santee had a great idea, and she put it into action. I'm only sorry that I didn't back her more firmly at the presentation. And I hereby publicly apologize for that, Marlo."

She gave him a brief smile, but she barely heard what he said. The last picture was still in her lap, and she knew she had to look at it.

"We're going to go with your campaign, Marlo," Art said. "We'll need a new model, but that shouldn't be all that difficult."

Jeri gave a little snort, but hardly anyone noticed. Marlo looked down at the last picture, and a tiny cry escaped her. Hardly anyone noticed that, either, because Grayson was shouting at them all, telling them they should all be as lucky as to have Marlo's logic, backbone and sense of innovation.

The picture was an enlargement of Cal's face. His blue eyes were gazing steadily at the camera, but a strong light from the side had caught the flash of his humor, and his mouth was tilted in a slow cowboy grin. Marlo stared at the picture, stared at the man she loved, and seemed to melt into her chair.

It was all there, his warmth, his strength, his stubbornness. How she loved him! She wished she could reach into the picture and pull him out. Putting her hand on the paper, she caressed his cheek, and tears filled her eyes.

How could she have been so stupid? How could she have gone on this long, not facing how much she loved him, how sterile her life was without him? Joy, the joy that had been missing from her days, began to grow inside her like a huge bubble about to burst.

Angel had been watching what she was going through, and he bent near her. "Well, what are you going to do, girl?" he asked her kindly.

She felt as though she would never catch her breath again. She turned and looked at her friend while fat, shimmery drops slid down her cheeks. "Go to him?" she asked.

"Sounds good to me. But then I've always been a sucker for true love."

"Marlo Santee," Mr. Grayson was saying, "I'm giving you back the Caron account. Your work on the olives and the toys proves what a mistake I made taking you off in the first place. Mr. Caron will be here at nine in the morning to meet with you."

It was all she'd ever dreamed of. Triumph was hers. She was exonerated and praised. They thought she had the golden touch. They wanted her. All eyes were watching, and they all said the same thing. "You're good, Marlo. We know that now. We want you to do good work and bring good things to all of us who work with you. We need you. We appreciate you."

There it was, in all their faces. She couldn't have asked for more. But it wasn't enough.

No, it wasn't enough. In fact, it hardly meant a thing anymore. Her eyes had been opened, and she knew what she really wanted. Oh, sure, success was nice. But without love it was hollow.

Marlo was trembling all over. She stood, clutching the picture that had made up her mind. "I'm sorry, Mr. Grayson," she said, and her voice was loud and clear. "I won't be here."

Grayson frowned. He didn't like being upstaged. "What are you talking about?"

"I—I have to quit." She began backing toward the door to the room. "I'm sorry I can't give two weeks' notice, but I just can't." She stopped in the doorway and looked back at them all. "Let Ted and Jeri handle it," she suggested. "I think they could do fine." She smiled tremulously. "Goodbye, everyone." And then she slipped out while they were all still too stunned to stop her.

"Good luck, honey," Phillipa called as she sped through the outer office. "You go get him."

Marlo laughed a little hysterically. Why was it everyone seemed to know all about her private life? But right now she didn't care. All she wanted was to get to Cal as quickly as possible. There was so much time to make up for.

13

THE SETTING SUN HUNG like an orange ball in the sky as she raced up the coast, but it was dark by the time she turned inland north of Santa Barbara. She'd stopped by her apartment to throw a few things into a case and to pull on gray slacks and a pearly-pink sweater, then had run out again, ignoring her ringing telephone.

"He's not here," Waco had told her when she'd skidded to a stop at the ranch in the Antelope Valley. He walked toward her, shaking his head. "He's been up in Paso Robles ever since that week he was with you."

"Do you think—should I go up after him?" she'd asked.

"He can be a stubborn cuss, but if anyone can roust him out of it, it'd be you, little lady."

She'd kissed him again, just as she'd done when he'd told her how to cook chili. "Thank you, Waco," she had called as she had run back to her car. Then she had come to another screeching halt in the dust. "But I don't know how to find him up there!"

He'd given her such detailed instructions that, even though she was driving through unfamiliar territory, she was confident. She whizzed through Buellton, bypassing the famous split pea soup restaurant even though she was starving, and forged ahead, her headlights cutting the night like lasers.

Santa Maria, Nipomo, Arroyo Grande, out to the coast again at Pismo Beach and inland again to the charming mission town of San Luis Obispo. The sign read twenty miles to Paso Robles before she finally realized just exactly what she was doing. The realization made her pull over to the side of the road and try to get her breathing under control.

He'd accused her of using him, of caring more for business, of sacrificing everything to ambition. He'd been angry. He probably thought she wasn't much better than Janice, who slept with people to advance her career. And he'd said he wasn't a forgiving man. What made her think he was going to welcome her with open arms?

He'd said he believed in trying for Utopia, and then he'd said he was sorry their value systems weren't the same. In other words, she had no integrity. It had made her angry at the time, but now she realized he had reason to say that. She'd spent so many years—all her life, really—trying to be good at something in order to be loved. Her entire sense of self-worth was tied up in her ambition. And then it had been ambition that had lost her the love she needed so badly. She saw that now. Would he believe she'd changed?

Swallowing hard, she started up the car again and nosed it out onto the highway. She followed the instructions Waco had given her and turned off after the little white church, taking a side road for three more miles. And then there it was—Stone Acres.

The house was set back on a rise. Its white pillars gleamed in the moonlight. It was a mansion fit for a Southern plantation novel, with a huge arched entryway. She half expected to hear the music from *Gone*

With the Wind wafting through the trees. It was thoroughly intimidating. She stopped the car and closed her eyes, trying to still her beating heart.

Her knees were like rubber as she made her way shakily to the front door. She pushed the bell. A dog barked somewhere, only to be hushed by a masculine voice. And then the door was opening.

The light from inside flooded out over her, and in the middle stood Cal. He was taller than she'd remembered, broader in the shoulders. His sandy hair curled about his head, and his blue eyes glowed like liquid stars.

"I must be dreaming," he said in a voice as smooth and rich as brandy.

All her well-thought-out plans of declaring her love deserted her. He was so gorgeous and so scary. She managed a wavery smile. "Only if you think you're looking at Scarlett O'Hara," she said. "Actually, it's only me."

"Only you," he repeated. There was a glow in his face, but she couldn't read it. She had no idea if he were pleased to see her or not.

"I was—I was just passing through and thought I'd drop in and see how you were doing," she lied shamelessly. "Quite well, it looks like." She waved at the opulent trappings.

"I'm fine," he said dryly. "Why don't you come on in and have a drink?"

She hoped her smile didn't look as sickly as she felt. "Why not?"

The inside of the place was more intimidating than the exterior. Thick carpets, textured wallpaper, sculptured cherry-wood furniture and huge oil paintings made it look as though it indeed belonged to one of the richest families in the world. A huge, wide, curving staircase led to the second story. *If he'd brought me here instead of the Antelope Valley, I'd have realized right away,* Marlo thought as he led her into the den. She had a new dread. He wouldn't think she'd come back because he was rich, would he?

"Here you are." He handed her a mixed drink, and she didn't even ask what it was. Two quick sips and she remembered that she hadn't eaten all day.

"Would you like to sit down?" he asked quietly.

His eyes were in shadows, and she couldn't read his expression. That made her very nervous. She wondered if he were trying to think of a tactful way to get rid of her. Well, too bad! She'd come this far. She was going to let him know how she felt, even if he didn't want to hear it. Just as soon as she got her nerve up. "No, thanks," she said, looking around a bit desperately. "I'd rather walk around and look at your things. May I?"

"Of course."

She went to the bookcase and ran her hand over the leather bindings, totally blind to the titles. How was she going to do this? He was so near and yet so far. She longed to run into his arms, but his silence was too imposing.

"How have things been, Marlo?" he asked, and she wondered briefly if he used the same cold tone for Janice when she came to call.

"Oh, things have been really good," she replied, turning to look at the porcelain collection behind glass. "I lost the Caron account, of course, but I've done really well on some other things, and now Art's offered the Caron account back to me."

That was a mistake. She could see right away what Cal thought. He drew himself up, and the cold black storm began to rage in his eyes again. Before he had a chance to accuse her of coming up to try to get him to model again, she went on hurriedly. "Don't worry! I'm not here about that. In fact, I turned him down." She took another sip of her drink and shrugged grandly. "I quit."

"You quit." She could see he was surprised. "When did you do that?"

"Oh—" she glanced at her watch "—about six hours ago."

The silence was deafening. She gulped down more of her drink, holding back the sputter in her throat. Finally he spoke again. "What are you planning to do?"

She found a glass case full of beautiful mineral specimens and crystals, and she leaned down to gaze inside. "Actually, I thought I'd try running my own ad office in some small town." She'd played with the idea ever since Angel had planted the seed in her mind, but not seriously. Suddenly it seemed a wonderful plan. She looked around the room. "Have you got any idea if Paso Robles has much of an advertising community?"

"I don't know if you'd be comfortable in Paso Robles. You'll never get rich and famous here."

Rich and famous had never been her goal. Didn't he know that? Love was all she wanted, all she'd ever wanted.

"And I suppose you'd rather I went someplace else, is that it?" she heard herself ask. She winced, turning away. No, no, this wasn't the way to do it. She wasn't going to get anywhere if this turned into a fight.

His voice was defensive, which was just what she'd asked for with her ridiculous accusation. "You can go where you like. It's all the same to me."

Her heart cracked within her. All the same to him. She'd been a fool to come up here in the middle of the night. He knew why she was here, and he was rejecting her. Something deep inside began to shake, and she bit her lip and reached for the edge of the desk to steady herself.

Her eyes focused on the pad of paper by the telephone. There was something familiar about the number she saw scrawled there. She looked again. It was her own telephone number, complete with area code. It had been copied time and time again, outlined and doodled around, and then someone had snapped the pencil into halves and left the two parts scattered across the page. She stared at the sight for a long moment before she fully comprehended what it must mean. Looking up, she found Cal's gaze on her. He'd seen her notice, and he was waiting for her reaction.

"Why didn't you go ahead and call me?" she asked, her voice the sound of metal scraping on wood.

"Because I'm a fool," he said so softly she thought at first she hadn't heard right.

The liquor must have gone to her head because she was suddenly very brave. She put herself squarely in front of the man she loved and looked him in the eye.

"Listen, cowboy," she said evenly. "I didn't drive all the way up here to play more guessing games with you. I've tried living without you, and it hasn't been good. I—" Her voice was choked, and suddenly her eyes filled with tears. "I love you, and I want to be with you. If you don't want me around, just say so . . ."

She couldn't see very well. His face was swimming in the mist of her tears, and all she saw was movement. But then he had her in his arms, and she didn't have to see anymore.

"Not want you! My God, woman, I've done nothing since we met but want you."

His body was hard and warm and wonderful, and she felt as though she were spinning in space. "But you don't trust me," she managed to say. "Can you forgive me for trying to get you to do the ads when it was uncomfortable for you? Can you forgive me for . . ."

He was holding her so tightly she could barely breathe. "Hush," he growled, his voice strained and broken. "Don't say one more word."

She blinked and felt blindly for his face with her hand. Was he crying? She must be hallucinating.

"Marlo, Marlo," he went on raggedly, holding her close as though she were something he cherished. "I'm such a stupid bastard. There's nothing to forgive you for. I'm the one who screwed up."

She felt awfully light-headed. "Really?"

"Yes, really." He buried his face in her hair and breathed deeply. "I let old hurts come between us, things that had nothing to do with you. I'd used them as a shield against involvement for so long that I couldn't seem to remember how to do anything else."

"You were reluctant from the first," she agreed, luxuriating in his embrace. "I could tell you didn't want to get involved with me. But I made you. Do you still resent that?"

"Never. I was just afraid of being used again, and I held back more than I should have. And after my stupid dramatic exit, it was hard to figure out how to come back into your life again without looking like a fool."

She touched his face. "I would never use you, Cal. I only want what's best for you. Except for one thing." She paused, smiling through her tears. "I want you to love me."

He laughed softly, rocking her in his arms and letting her hair spill about his face. "You smell like life. Do you know that? I feel as though I've been dead without you. I love you, Marlo. I've loved you from that night I rubbed baking soda on your sunburn and then watched you sleep with the morning sun on your beautiful face. I should have told you then. I should have grabbed you and brought you here and forced you to listen to reason."

"Reason?" She was laughing through her tears. "You big oaf, what does reason have to do with it?"

"Not much," he agreed, nibbling her neck. "In fact," he breathed against her satiny skin, "I think reason is receding as we speak." He tasted the edge of her chin and groaned, his hands slipping down to find the curve of her bottom. "And good riddance," he murmured.

"Oh, Cal," she sighed, leaning back in his arms. "I've missed you so."

His lips caught hers, moving greedily, nipping and pulling, while she opened her mouth to invite him inside. "Marlo," he sighed, his breath mingling with hers, "you've got my soul in your hands. You can do what you want with me."

Her answering laugh was cut short as his mouth covered hers, and she sank into the magic once again, the sweet, intoxicating magic that only this rough man could produce. His tongue curled and uncurled, challenging hers and then retreating, until she was moaning in frustrated urgency, and then he plunged in to satisfy both their hunger. Her fingers kneaded compulsively through the fabric of his shirt, digging into his hardness in a primitive female response. His hands were at the belt of her slacks, pulling them open.

"You don't know," he muttered against her trembling lips, "how starved I am for the feel of your body."

"Oh, I know," she said with a gasp as he slid the slacks down off her hips. "Believe me, I know." Her fingers curled around the lapels of his shirt, tugging to open the fabric and give her access to the dark, solid wall of his chest.

The slacks were in a pool around her ankles, and she kicked them away along with her shoes, while Cal began rolling her sweater up, his hands rubbing across her ribs to find the fullness above.

"You have the most beautiful breasts I've ever seen," he told her huskily as they swung free from the confinement of soft wool. Leaning down, he caught a nipple with his tongue.

She'd never been particularly body conscious or proud of her shape, but right now she felt like the most beautiful woman in the world. "All for you," she crooned, her eyes half closed with drowsy desire.

When they were both naked, she expected him to pull her down onto the thickly carpeted floor, but instead he swung her up into his arms.

"Where are we going?" she asked, blinking in the golden light.

"Where do you think, Scarlett?" he teased, licking her ear. "I'm going to carry you up the staircase, *Gone With the Wind*-style."

She chuckled. "How romantic. And how fitting." She looked up into his face. "You've even got the mustache for it."

"And you've got the hair for it," he added as her long black tresses swept across his shoulder. He started out of the den, carrying her easily, and she snuggled happily in his arms until she caught sight of the picture they made in the hall mirror.

"But I'm not dressed for it," she wailed. "Scarlett had a long, flowing gown that swept across the stairs."

"No problem." He put her down and strode quickly to the window, grabbing a filmy sheer panel from beneath the heavy draperies and tearing it free with one clean jerk. "I seem to remember that Scarlett was a resourceful lady," he said. "How's this?"

She stared openmouthed as he wrapped the lovely fabric around her shoulders. "Cal, you're ripping your house apart!"

His grin was arrogantly endearing. "I'm ripping my life apart, lovely lady. And all to fit you inside it."

He swung her up into his arms again, and this time she couldn't complain about the lack of flowing material. He carried her up the staircase, and she closed her eyes, reveling in the strength of his arms. When he laid her gently on his bed, she looked up and reached for the man she loved, the man she was going to cling to forever. Slowly he unwound the lacy cloth from around her and revealed the prize he'd won. And his touch, his arousing hands and lips, taught her that love was indeed mutual.

When he slid up between her long legs and entered her, she arched a joyous welcome, crying out as they rose together into the heat of ultimate passion, clinging to him with all her strength, growling her intense response to his thrusts and crying quiet tears as they lay together in the aftermath.

"What's the matter?" he whispered, touching one tear, then another.

"I—I just love you so much," she whispered back. "And I was so afraid I'd lost you."

"Never."

"But . . . if I hadn't come up to find you tonight . . ."

He put a wet finger to her lips. "Take a look at this." He rolled over and pulled open a drawer in the bedside table, taking out some papers and tossing them onto the bed. Raising herself on one elbow, she picked them up.

"Two air tickets to Hawaii," he explained. "One in your name, one in mine."

The travel date was on the coming weekend. She looked up at him questioningly, tears still in her eyes.

"I didn't know quite how," he told her sheepishly, "but I was going to get you on that plane."

"You were going to kidnap me?"

"If I had to. All I wanted was a week away from everything to convince you that you needed me."

She threw down the tickets, laughing. "Oh goody. When does the convincing begin?"

He pretended to look hurt. "You mean you didn't notice? What do you think we were just doing?"

She lay back against the pillows in a seductive pose. "Mere hors d'oeuvres," she teased. "I'm waiting for the main course."

A dangerous light spiced his gaze. "You are, are you?" His voice was low and promising. "Throw out the silverware, honey," he growled as he rose above her. "For this you'll need both hands."

He came down on the bed like a predator on its prey, and she screamed, rolling away and laughing at the same time, trying to get away, but not very hard.

"What do you think you're doing?" she cried.

"Be quiet," he ordered, pulling her back underneath him. "Did Scarlett talk back to Rhett Butler?"

"You bet she did!"

"Well, then, talk all you want," he said into the hollow of her neck. "But leave the rest to me."

She loved the man. She was ready to spend the rest of her life loving him. And he convinced her she was right to want that. Time after time.

THE SHRILL SOUND of a telephone woke them in the morning. Cal reached for it groggily, then handed the receiver to her.

"It's your boss," he said, pulling himself up against the pillows as she put the receiver to her ear.

Her boss. Her mind was still too heavy with sleep to think clearly. Who was her boss and what did he want?

"Marlo!" Art Grayson's voice barked at her. "Marlo, is that you?"

Marlo groaned. "Mr. Grayson—"

"It's Art, Art! I keep telling you."

"Mr. Grayson, you woke me up."

"It's ten o'clock. It's about time somebody woke you up. You're late for work."

Work. Her brain was finally clearing. She looked over at Cal and smiled good morning. He leaned down and kissed her on the lips while Grayson continued to scream from the receiver. The kiss lasted a long time. It tasted like musky wine. Sighing, she finally drew away and put the phone to her ear again.

"Mr. Grayson, how did you get this number?" she asked.

"Ted found it for me."

"Ted?"

"Yes. I told him to find you or lose his job, so he did it."

Marlo giggled and stretched under the sheet, enjoying the feel of her naked body against the cool linen. "I'll bet he loved that."

"Who cares what Ted loves? I didn't call to talk about him. I want you back. Take a few days off, if you want, but I want you back on Monday."

She yawned. "Sorry, Mr. Grayson. I can't make it. I'm going to be busy." She watched, eyes half closed, as Cal began to peel away the sheet and explore the creamy texture of her skin.

"Busy?" Art blustered. "Busy doing what?"

Cal's lips were finding intimate spots that quivered to his touch, and she had to hold back a gasp. "I'm getting married, Mr. Grayson. I'm sorry I can't invite you, but it's going to be such a small wedding—"

"You can't get married! You've got to handle the Caron account!"

Could one really make love all night and then all day, too? Well, why not? "Sorry," she sighed.

"Listen." His voice got crafty. "I'll make you a vice president. How's that? The youngest vice president we've ever had!"

She reached to tug the sheet away from Cal, too, so that she could see every inch of his marvelous golden body. "I'm sorry, Mr. Grayson. I'm afraid I've had a better offer."

"I'll double your salary!"

She put a hand over the receiver and looked at Cal. "He wants to double my salary and make me a vice president," she said calmly.

Cal pretended to consider. "I'll give you laundry to do and babies to wash," he countered. "And lots of lusty love."

She sighed again. "I'm sorry, Mr. Grayson. I've had an offer I can't refuse."

Grayson's angry shouts were becoming repetitive, and the man in bed with her was getting more persuasive. She giggled. "I'm going to have to go now, Mr. Grayson," she told him breathlessly. "I've got to take care of business. Bye."

She pushed the phone away and turned to her man. "I told him we were getting married."

He leaned down to take the lobe of her ear between his teeth. "We are," he mumbled.

"But you haven't really asked me yet."

He leaned back and gazed into her laughing eyes. "Marlo Santee, will you marry me?" he demanded.

"California James, I'd be delighted."

"Good," he growled, returning to the task at hand. "Now on with the honeymoon."

"I love you so much," she sighed.

He bit her ear and grinned. "Good. Because frankly, my dear, I do give a damn."

Harlequin Temptation

COMING NEXT MONTH

Harlequin "Super Celebration" SWEEPSTAKES

NEW PRIZES—NEW PRIZE FEATURES & CHOICES—MONTHLY

1. To enter the sweepstakes, follow the instructions outlined on the Center Insert Card. Alternate means of entry, NO PURCHASE NECESSARY, you may also enter by mailing your name, address and birthday on a plain 3" x 5" piece of paper to: In U.S.A.: Harlequin "Super Celebration" Sweepstakes, P.O. Box 1867, Buffalo, N.Y. 14240-1867. In Canada: Harlequin "Super Celebration" Sweepstakes, P.O. Box 2800, 5170 Yonge Street, Postal Station A, Willowdale, Ontario M2N 6J3.

2. Winners will be selected in random drawings from all entries received. All prizes will be awarded. These prizes are in addition to any free gifts which might be offered. Versions of this sweepstakes with different prizes may appear in other presentations by TorStar and their affiliates. The maximum value of the prizes offered is $8,000.00. Winners selected will receive the prize offered from their prize package.

3. The selection of winners will be conducted under the supervision of Marden-Kane, an independent judging organization. By entering the sweepstakes, each entrant accepts and agrees to be bound by these rules and the decision of the judges which shall be final and binding. Odds of winning are dependent upon the total number of entries received. Taxes, if any, are the sole responsibility of the winners. Prizes are not transferable. This sweepstakes is scheduled to appear in Retail Outlets of Harlequin Books during the period of June 1986 to December 1986. All entries must be received by January 31st, 1987. The drawing will take place on or about March 1st, 1987 at the offices of Marden-Kane, Lake Success, New York. For Quebec (Canada) residents, any litigation regarding the running of this sweepstakes and the awarding of prizes must be submitted to La Regie de Lotteries et Course du Quebec.

4. This presentation offers the prizes as illustrated on the Center Insert Card.

5. This offer is open to residents of the U.S., and Canada, 18 years or older, except employees of TorStar, its affiliates, subsidiaries, Marden-Kane and all other agencies and persons connected with conducting this sweepstakes. All Federal, State and local laws apply. Void where prohibited or restricted by law. Winners will be notified by mail and may be required to execute an affidavit of eligibility and release which must be returned within 14 days after notification. Winners consent to the use of their name, photograph and/or likeness for advertising and publicity in conjunction with this and similar promotions without additional compensation. One prize per family or household. Canadian winners will be required to answer a skill testing question.

6. For a list of our most recent prize winners, send a stamped, self-addressed envelope to: WINNERS LIST, c/o Marden-Kane, P.O. Box 525, Sayreville, NJ 08872.

No Lucky Number needed to win!